GUNS OF ABRAHAM

Seth Driskill

Guns of Abraham
Copyright © 2017, Seth Driskill

All rights reserved. No part of this book may be reproduced or transmitted in any form or by any means without written permission from the author.

ISBN 978-0-9984318-2-6

Gideon, Maug, Black Label, and all other "Lost Titan" properties belong to

C.L. Williams.

Ryan Martel and Darren Gresham

belong to Trey Stewart

Firefly belongs to Lydia Lyle

For Best Reading Experience, First Read:

THE REDEEMERS
vol. 1

AND

THIS BOOK
DEDICATED TO
THE ECCENTRIC FAN

Preface: Chase Williams, a former Redeemer, has formed a team of gunslingers, *The Guns of Abraham*. With the help of a new friend, Gridd, they discover that Brassport is actually a city located in the dimension between space colony Jettahawk and the Earth they live on. They must go to Brassport and recover the lost Power Diamond as well as find Ronin Torchwood and bring him to justice.

Table of Contents

Previously in The Master Series 8

Prologue 9

Bullet Storm 23

Masquerade 55

New Brassport City 64

Letter to the Reader 106

The Lost Titan 107

Torchwood Trials 123

Triggermate's Adventure 184

Maverick's Malice 195

Emissary 201

The Truth of Judgement Day 242

Previously in The Master Series

Drake Barrows, a.k.a. *The Redeemer*, and his team of powered individuals known as *The Redeemers*, successfully eradicated The Royale, a corrupt organization committed to mayhem. They did this through an elaborate plan aptly referred to as *Judgment Day*. The plan was to trap all of The Royale within a huge nuclear blast-proof cylinder in a deserted area near Brassport. Once this was accomplished, a nuclear bomb was dropped, destroying all that was left of The Royale. Chase Williams, son of Abraham Williams, along with many of the other Redeemers, was able to escape this blast with the help of their ally, Dawn. But, the rescue came at a high price.

Shortly after warping the team to safety, Dawn died from a battle-inflicted wound. Dawn's blood is on the hands of the evil titan Ronin Torchwood. The team leader, Drake Barrows, seemingly died as well, but was later revealed to still be alive. Chase left The Redeemers before this truth was known, and still lives without the knowledge of Drake's survival. He now leads *The Guns of Abraham*. For the past few months he has pursued the combined forces that operate at the direction of Ronin Torchwood, in order to discover his whereabouts as well as the location of the Power Diamond. Torchwood's combined force is made up of the *Valorack* and the *Psychonauts*. Chase Williams and his team of nine will stop at nothing to bring Torchwood to justice.

Prologue

On the outskirts of Fair Grove lives a man named Abraham Williams, with his wife Karen. Their son Chase and his cousin, Gideon Maverick, live with them, but are out for the night. This particular night, something is off. Evil is approaching and Abraham knows it.

Abraham: Karen... Karen get up! They're here.

Abraham fumbles through the house as he takes his startled wife by the hand and leads her to the bunker he built beneath his house.

Karen: What's happening. Did... they find out?

Abraham looks his wife in the eyes as he holds her face in his hands.

Abraham: Stay here. Don't make a sound. I'll fix this. I'll protect us. I promise.

Abraham turns and leaves the bunker, shutting the door behind him as he hears his wife call out.

Karen: Honey wait! Don't leave!

Abraham runs back into the house and dives into the closest room as bullets begin to rip through the house from the attackers outside.

He opens a nearby safe and removes a handgun, then immediately throws his back against the wall.

Bullets continue to pierce the house, tearing through the furniture and cabinets. All he can hear is glass shattering and wood splintering.

Suddenly, all goes quiet. Abraham peers around the corner, still holding the handgun near his chest, not daring to venture out. The silence sends warning that a bigger threat is approaching.

The door shatters open and five men wearing red robes and white masks with small circular openings at the eyes and mouth enter the bullet-withered house.

A tall menacing figure wearing a black robe and gold and black mask walks in. This is the one known as the Master Royale, leader of the The Royale.

Abraham: *(whispering to himself in disbelief)* The Royale… They're here… But how?

Master Royale: Search the house. The Power Diamond is in here somewhere.

The Royale gunmen spread throughout the house and begin overturning everything in a frantic search for the diamond.

One of the gunmen starts to make his way into the room where Abraham is hiding. As soon as he steps foot in the room, Abraham sweeps his leg, sending him crashing to the floor. With one loud crack, Abraham punches the man in the face as he lays on the ground, shattering his mask.

Master Royale: Ah… Mr. Williams… Good to see you. May we have a moment of your time?

The remaining four Royale members lunge toward him as he holds his gun ready to fire.

Abraham: Get out of my house, you filth!

Abraham shoots with incredible accuracy as he takes out two of the men. The third man fires a round through Abraham's leg, causing him to hit the ground hard.

Master Royale: Bring him here.

The remaining gunmen pick the wounded man up and drag him before the Master Royale.

Master Royale: Where is the *diamond*, Abraham? As you can see, I'm not very patient today.

Abraham's leg continues to seep blood as he lays on the ground.

Abraham: I'll never tell you! That diamond is too powerful for someone as weak as you to handle.

Abraham spits on the ground in disgust, close to the man's feet.

He hears his wife's scream getting louder and louder as Royale members drag her into the room. They throw her next to him. Abraham's face winces in pain, partly from the open wound in his leg, partly from the thought of The Royale using his wife to make him talk.

Abraham: Karen what happened? How did they find you?

Karen: I'm sorry, I tried to fight back! They... They found the diamond...

Her voice trails off, as she begins to realize the implications of what she just said.

Abraham looks down in complete dismay as he hears the words he hoped to never hear. He looks up to see a Royale member handing the diamond to their attacker.

Royale Member: It was locked away in the bunker beneath the house.

The red diamond radiates a bright color throughout the house. Abraham holds his wife close as he looks down to see his blood blending with the color of the diamond's light.

Master Royale: Look at this! Oh, it's beautiful. Ha Ha! How did you think you could keep something this magnificent away from me?

He says this menacingly as he places the diamond in a metal pressurized container by his side.

Master Royale: Bring in the *Sentry*.

Karen begins to sob heavily as she places her head on Abraham's side.

They both know that this is most likely the end for them.

Suddenly a loud noise breaks throughout the house as a tall machine-looking sentinel enters...

Master Royale: This is one of my top men. We call him the Royale Sentry, and tonight, his will be the last face you see.

The mech suited man prepares his shoulder gun to fire. The barrel begins to spin sending a warning that the end has come.

Abraham: I love you Karen. I'm sorry I couldn't save you... I'm...

Karen: Be strong... We tried our best. The rest is up to...

Karen's sentence is cut short as the Sentry sends a flurry of bullets through her body.

Abraham: NOOOOO!

Abraham quickly prepares to meet his fate as well when suddenly a voice shouts out.

Royale Gunman: STOP! Wait!

The gunman dives in front of Abraham and the Sentry quickly stops firing, narrowly avoiding harming one of his own men.

Royale Sentry: What is this? You're interfering!

Abraham holds his wife's lifeless body in his arms and begins to weep loudly.

Royale Gunman: Why do we have to kill them? We have the diamond... Can't we just... leave them?

The gunman's voice is that of youth, maybe a teenage boy – suddenly afraid for his life as he regrets this impulse reaction.

Master Royale: Boy. Step forward. Tell me your name.

He obeys and steps toward his superior.

Royale Gunman: My name is Michael... sir. Michael Barrows.

The Master Royale smacks the kid hard and sends his mask flying across the room, revealing the face of a very timid, brown-haired boy.

Master Royale: Ah yes. I remember you. *You're weak.* There is no place in The Royale for someone who is weak.

Michael: I'm sorry sir! I won't let it happen again, I promise. I should have never questioned your orders.

The Master Royale places his hand on the kid's shoulder and forces a gun into his right hand.

Master Royale: Prove yourself. Finish the job for me. Prove that you're worth my time, Michael.

The boy shakes as he holds the gun in his hands, slowly turning to face Abraham.

Michael: You want me to...

Master Royale: Yes idiot. I want you to kill him! He wronged us. This diamond can power entire cities with clean, untraceable energy and he wanted to keep it all to himself! That's punishable by death, don't you think?

Abraham: Don't listen to him. He's trying to control you... You don't have to do this!

Michael begins to shake more as tears stream down his face.

Michael: I don't have a choice!

Abraham: You always have a choice. He doesn't have to own you! You can escape this! But if you pull that trigger, he wins.

Master Royale: What's it going to be kid. Don't defile my name. I saved you... Don't you remember? You and your brother owe everything to me!

Michael, closing his eyes for a moment, takes a deep breath and his shaking stops. Then he looks down at Abraham with rage-filled eyes as he aims the gun directly at his chest.

Michael: You will not stop The Royale! We will prevail!

Abraham forces all the energy he has left in his body to stand up. His leg still is dripping blood as he slowly limps over to Michael. He stands only a few feet away as Michael backs up.

Abraham: Then do it kid. I won't back down. But you better look me in the eyes and remember this moment. The moment you decided to be a slave to evil.

The kid trembles a bit as Abraham says this. He looks down at Karen's dead body and starts to consider his action.

Michael: I am a slave to no one!

Michael pulls the trigger and the bullet pierces through Abraham's stomach. This knocks him back a few feet but Abraham still powers forward even with this second bullet wound.

Master Royale: Step aside Michael, he's a tough one to crack I see. We'll finish this.

Michael drops the gun and runs to the Master Royale's side as Abraham continues to limp forward.

Master Royale: On my command! READY! FIRE!

The Sentry unloads his shoulder gun as bullets rip through Abraham's body. Blood splatters from his back as he, with one final lunge forward, falls to the ground.

Abraham looks up at the Sentry as the men around him start to pour gasoline around the house.

He gasps for air through his pierced lungs and forces out whispered words as the Sentry looks down on him.

Abraham: You... will... never... win.

The Sentry scoffs as he exits the house.

The Master Royale speaks over the COM system within his mask.

Master Royale: Tell Gladstone to stop the mining in Egypt. We have the diamond.

He turns to Michael, who at this point looks very shaken up but eerily content with his action.

Master Royale: I see greatness in you Michael. I might just make you into something powerful one day.

Michael looks up at his leader and smiles menacingly.

Master Royale: Get everyone out of here, then light the place up. We have an announcement to make back at headquarters.

Everyone leaves the house. All that's left is Abraham's bleeding body as he grasps to what little life he has left.

He slowly drags himself towards the open door of his house as flames start to engulf the walls around him. He tries desperately to escape but he eventually gives up as he has no strength, no life, left in his body. The flames approach him faster and faster as he feels the heat radiate off of them. He looks back one last time to see his wife, laying there dead.

Abraham: I'll see you soon Karen. I'll see... you soon...

Abraham closes his eyes, ready to accept his fate.

Suddenly, he feels the warmth of the flames move farther and farther away as he feels the cold air brush over his face from outside. Someone was pulling him out of the burning house.

It was his son, Chase.

Chase: Dad! Dad what happened! You're bleeding so much! What should I do!

Abraham: Son... It's okay... Look at me.

Chase comes close to his dad with tear stained eyes as his cousin, Gideon, and his close friend Tristen stand behind him. Abraham fights to stay conscious, only able to whisper as life quickly escapes his grasp.

Abraham: Listen to my words... carefully. Stay in Fair Grove, protect this land. They'll... come back...

Chase: Who... Who will come back!?

Tristen: Who did this?

Abraham: I... don't have any time left. Take my necklace.

Chase removes the blood-stained necklace from his father and holds it in his hand. Attached to it is a bullet, a chain-link, and a key. On one side of the key is an Image of a bird and on the other side is a cage.

Abraham: Do... you... remember what... I told you those things... represent?

Chase quickly recites the answer.

Chase: The chain is a reminder of the bondage I've been set free from. The bondage of my own evil desires. The key is a reminder that I'm only one bad decision away from being trapped by the consequences of my actions.

Chase tries hard to continue talking as he is overcome with sorrow and tears.

Chase: ...And the bullet is a reminder to always make war against those who would harm others.

Abraham smiles as his son says this.

Abraham: Good... Good son. Never Ever Forget!

Chase: I won't dad. I promise I won't but... but what do I do now? Where do I go without you!

Abraham: You must fight... You must make war... You must never... stop, until the evil that caused this is... brought to justice! People will try to stop you... People will do all they can to keep you... from succeeding... but you must... always... make... war.

Chase looks angry as he stares into his dad's eyes one final time.

Abraham: You must... bring forth... redemption.

Abraham breathes out his last breath as he holds Chase's hand and gently lays his head against the dry sediment beneath him.

Chase closes his eyes and screams out a loud shout of brokenness that rings throughout the outskirts of Fair Grove. Rage. Piercing sorrow. A cry for justice. War.

He opens his eyes to see that it is morning. The house he once lived in lays before him. A pile of scorched rubble. He looks down to see that he's lying in Gideon's convertible sports car.

Chase: What... What happened. How is it morning?

Chase looks around frantically to see that Gideon and Tristen are gone. Suddenly he hears Tristen's voice shout out from the distance.

Tristen: Chase!

Tristen runs over to Chase and helps him up.

Tristen: You blacked out last night. The fire department came and put out the fire and the authorities took your parents... well... bodies away.

Chase looks confused as his eyes adjust to the morning's light.

Chase: If I blacked out? How am I still here? Why didn't they take me to a hospital or something?

Tristen: Gideon went on a rampage. He stole one of the cop cars and drove off and that kind of stole everyone's attention. Your vitals were fine and you started to wake up. They asked you a few questions and you answered clearly, so they decided you were good to go.

Chase doesn't answer for a while.

Tristen: Your uncle came by last night. He was devastated. You know how protective of his sister he is. He has custody of you now. Don't you remember any of this?

Chase: No... I don't remember a thing. Except... what he said to me.

Chase looks down at his father's necklace and his own blood-stained shirt.

Tristen: Your uncle is down in the bunker. There is something you need to see.

Chase: Bunker? We have a bunker?

Tristen looks shocked at this statement.

Tristen: Dude, how did you not... ah, you got to see this! Follow me!

Chase slowly steps out of the vehicle and fumbles over to an open bunker door with steps leading underground. The bunker door is covered in stone-work like the rest of the house, impossible to notice when closed.

He follows Tristen down to see his very overweight uncle, Gregory Thompson.

Chase is completely baffled as he looks around at this mysterious bunker fortified with weapons and ammo clustered throughout the walls.

Gregory: Hey kiddo, come take a look at this. Maybe it'll ease your mind a bit.

The heavy 400-pound man pats Chase on the back with a loud thud as he gestures towards the far wall of the bunker.

Against the wall are blueprints for three mech suits.

Chase walks up to the wall and looks closely at the designs.

On the left, there is a design for a metal suit with mechanized wings and two rapid fire handguns that seem to have spinning barrels, almost like a handheld Gatling gun. Under the design is the name "Tristen Hayes."

To the right is another design for an armored suit with big shoulder pads. Below is a design for a huge gun, the biggest Chase has ever seen. It looks like three miniguns attached to one big frame. Chase can only imagine the damage a weapon like that could do. Under these blueprints is the name "Gregory Thompson."

Chase steps back in shock as he sees his name in the middle. Above it, the blueprints for another mech suit. All the armor is well designed except for the place where the helmet should be. In the helmet's absence are written the words, "helmet design pending." Next to the suit are the designs for a machine gun with what appears to be a chainsaw attachment on the end.

Chase, Tristen, and Gregory look at these blueprints for a while without speaking.

Tristen: Why do you think he made these for us specifically? I mean, your dad and me were close, but there has to be more reason than that.

Gregory: It makes sense to me. I'm too big to be flying around, but I got the muscle to carry around a hefty gun like that. You seem to be the more agile type so flying around suits ya'.

Chase: So, are we going to build these things or what?

Gregory looks at Tristen and they both nod.

Tristen: It's what he would want. He said "make war," right? This looks like a great way to do just that.

Chase looks back at the blueprints again with a content smile on his face. Somewhere between the heart-wrenching loss of his parents and the parting words of his father, he finds his purpose beginning to take shape.

Gregory: We found this note on the table earlier. It's for you, bud.

Chase picks up the note and begins to read it.

The note says- Dear Chase,

I have designed these weapons for the ones I see fit to use them in my absence. My plan was to give these to you on your 16th birthday as a project we could both work on. If you're reading this, it means I'm not here and you're receiving this gift a little early. You're probably wondering why I've been designing firepower like this. It's because I have something that a lot of evil people want and one day, they'll come for it. I can't tell you what it is for the time being, just in case this note falls into the wrong hands. Chase, my son, you are strong, you are smart, and one day you will be a hero. Take these designs as my help to you in assembling a force against evil. They will come, they will attack, and you and your team will be there to stop them. I'm sure of it. I call these suits my "guns," if you will. The "Guns of Abraham," to be more specific. Don't give up son. Take these ideas that you see before you and make them a reality. Never stop fighting for the good that's left in this world. Always make war.

-Abraham.

Day 1

Bullet Storm

Three Years Later

Six Months after the events of Redeemers Vol. 1

The Guns of Abraham all lay hidden around the perimeter of a deep crater as they await the best opportunity to attack. Within the crater are their foes, members of the Valorack.

Chase Williams, the team leader, is fully suited in his new and improved mech suit. Even without the suit he is a strong, broad shouldered 19-year-old man with an iron will. He goes by the battle name Steampunk. Only the people who are closest to him call him by his real name. His brass-alloy armor shines in the sun as he prepares to attack. Next to his side is his trademark weapon, a fully automatic M1216 machine gun, tipped with a titanium alloy chainsaw. On his shoulder is mounted an M-134 six-barreled rotary minigun. Covering his face is the mask of the Royale Sentry who killed his parents years ago. Chase acquired this mask after defeating the man six months prior. He wears it as a reminder that he is fighting to end the evil that caused his parents demise. The mask is fully metal and covers his entire head. It has openings only at both eyes, and from the front of his head all of the way to the back are three mohawk like metal fins that jut out about an inch. Engraved on his shoulder plate is the phrase, "I fight in memory of Drake, and win until Dawn's return."

Chase - Steampunk - speaks into the COM system within his helmet to the team.

Steampunk: Okay let's get a head count. How many people are you seeing down there?

Slinger: They keep moving in and out of the tents so it's hard to keep track. I'd say at least 50 of them for now, though.

Hevy: Nah man. There's gotta be at least a hundred of 'em. Heh heh... This could be fun.

Slinger and Hevy are the oldest members of the Guns of Abraham. They helped start it years ago when Chase discovered his father's mech-suit blueprints. Slinger is Chase's best friend, Tristen Hayes, and Hevy is none other than Gregory Thompson. Gregory, Chase's uncle, has taken it upon himself to raise his nephew since his brother-in-law Abraham died.

Slinger is the aerial assaulter of the team. His suit allows him to attack from above. He lays in the crater next to Steampunk with his large brass-lattice wings deployed and ready to send him soaring. He wears a brown leather jacket and rugged tan colored cargo pants. Only the most critical parts of his attire are armored to reduce weight for flying. Pinned to the left of his chest is a gold colored gear with the letters "G O A," in the center - the official team crest of the "Guns of Abraham". In his hands are two rapid-fire handguns. Each gun's barrels spin fast and shoot *at the speed of a Gatling gun. Strapped along his belt is an arsenal of loaded clips for fast reloading.*

Hevy is a very large, grossly overweight man. He cannot run fast or maneuver well, but for what he lacks in speed, he gains in strength and firepower. On his back is a steam-powered jet pack that allows him to hover for a brief moment. His jet-pack also holds two heat tracking missiles that he can launch at will. His main weapon however, is something he calls "Barnstormer." It is a large frame that holds three rotating six-barreled miniguns together. When he fires these guns, an enormous flurry of destruction emits forward and obliterates everything in its path. The only limitation is that it can only be used in brief bursts before it has to cool down.

Jazz: They got about... let's see... 1... 2... 3... 4... 5 tanks on this side.

Contra: They got big tanks and we got big guns. Their guns? Well... Not so big.

Clang: Dude move over! I can't see.

Bolts: I have the binoculars, not you. Why do you need to see?

Steampunk: For the love of all things good! Why on earth are you arguing now of all times?

Jazz is the most unique of the group. Born and raised in Hawaii, his dream was to be a musician. He still is a musician at heart, but a marksman by trade. Next to him is an electric guitar. It's brass-colored to match the rest of the team's armor, and has engraved on it the same "Guns of Abraham" symbol that the team wears proudly. It's a McSwain "Machine Custom" industrial-age-themed guitar. Jazz's wardrobe is very casual but flashy. He wears a leather top hat, a black canvas jacket, and a ragged, torn, grey, loose fitting shirt that he should have thrown away years ago. Hanging from his side is an array of colorful bandanas tied together. His right hand is covered with a golden gauntlet with sharp tips at each finger.

Contra: So when do we strike? My trigger finger is getting twitchy.

Steampunk: Not yet. I'd like to actually plan an attack for once instead of just acting on impulse.

Contra: That's no fun.

Contra is a tall, muscular, militant brute of a man. His weapon of choice is a monstrous war hammer that he holds by his side. It's handle also serves as a bazooka when necessary. It can only fire once, but this one single shot can, most conveniently, destroy any collection of tanks in close proximity. Strapped to his back is the same model automatic shotgun as Steampunk's, but with no chainsaw. Contra is the one member of the team who looks out of place, as nothing he wears is brass or mimicking the appearance of the steam-powered industrial age. His wardrobe is a camouflaged tank top and grey pants. His steel-toed boots lay heavy on the ground as he waits for Steampunk's orders.

Bolts: Should I activate the whips yet?

Clang: No idiot! He just said to wait.

Bolts: I didn't ask you!

Steampunk: Keep it down!

Bolts and Clang are small in stature, but the two brothers pack a punch. Both of them are covered with bronze armor except for their heads. Each of them wear circular goggles to protect their eyes. Bolt's weapons are two metal wire whips that extend from leather-bound handles. With the press of a button, he can send a high-voltage jolt through the whips, stunning anything within their reach.

Clang's weapon is different. Below his hands are canons that emit a devastatingly low-bass sonic pulse that physically pushes enemies back, as well as destroys any fragile materials nearby. Above his hands are launchers that fire small explosive disks which detonate on impact.

Steampunk: Gold-bug, what do you and Hudson see?

Gold-bug: A bunch of unsuspecting Valorack scum.

Hudson: Yeah, they have no idea we're here.

Gold-bug is an average-sized 15-year-old boy who wears gold-alloy armor. Each piece of it is plate-like and resembles that of a beetle, thus giving him the name Gold-bug. These armored plates can connect together when he rolls up into a ball, making him somewhat of a cannonball. He can charge his attack up by spinning - and once released, he will launch forward and soar through the air like a bullet - crushing anything in his path. When he is not in cannonball form, he attacks with his two automatic handguns. They fire his trademark golden bullets.

Hudson: I've been meaning to ask you guys: Why don't I have a nickname? You all do, but I just go by Hudson.

Jazz: You've got to earn your nickname, bud. We don't just make them up on the spot. It has to be... I don't know... Inspired.

Hudson is the newest member of the Guns of Abraham. He joined the team shortly after Steampunk left The Redeemers, and has been training with them ever since. This is his first mission with the team. Hudson wears a mech suit much like Steampunk's. He designed the suit himself, but with Chase's help, has upgraded the original. His weapons are the same as Steampunk's, with both a shoulder minigun and an automatic machine gun. His gun does not have the chainsaw attachment either. That's reserved as a Steampunk trademark. For this mission, Hudson for some reason has a bucket strapped to his head as a helmet, with holes cut out where his eyes are.

Gold-bug: Hudson... Why is there a bucket on your head?

The rest of the team hears this over the COM and turns to look at Hudson.

Hevy: Ha Ha! What are you thinkin' kid?

Hudson: Well, I still haven't designed a helmet and I don't want my head to get blown off, so I had to improvise...

The entire team tries hard to hold back laughter.

Clang: Well, there's your new nickname man. From now on, you will be known as Bucket.

Again, the team laughs, but this time loudly.

Hudson: Hold up! Now that's not final, right?

Slinger: Oh... It's final... heh... Bucket.

The laughter grows without reservation.

Steampunk: Guys, stop talking! I think they've spotted us.

The team gets quiet immediately as they look down to see Valorack men pointing in their direction. Suddenly an alarm sounds and the base turns to chaos as they prepare to attack.

Steampunk: Well, so much for professionalism. Scratch the plan, just attack.

Bullets start to soar upwards as Slinger activates his mechanical wings and soars to the sky.

Clang: I thought that **was** the plan?

The rest of the team jumps from their hiding and makes their approach on the ground.

Hevy hits the ground with a quake-like thud, stopping the nearby Valoracks in their tracks. They stand confused as this large man holding an even larger gun towers before them.

Hevy: Now I know what you're thinkin'. How does a man my size fall out of the sky and not break his legs?

The stunned Valoracks just glare back at him, confused.

Hevy immediately begins firing the Barnstormer at the men, leaving them no time to respond before falling to the ground.

Hevy: Now you're thinking, "Ouch! I've been shot... a lot."

All Hevy can see before him is a barrage of bullets and smoke as he continues this display of firepower throughout the entire left wing of the base.

Hevy: What? I... I can't hear ya' over the sound of me winning!

Slinger soars overhead and maneuvers his way through the endless enemy gunfire and explosions.

Slinger: Gold-bug, follow me to that tank!

Gold-bug: On it!

Gold-bug curls himself into a ball and starts spinning in place rapidly. He finally releases this charge and storms across the terrain at a break-neck pace, looking more like low-level cannon fire than a human.

Slinger begins firing at enemies below as he makes his way to the moving tank ahead.

Gold-bug powers across the terrain at incredible speed as he ricochets off of unsuspecting Valorack. He eventually rolls up the side of a mound and soars into the air towards Slinger.

Slinger: Watch out man! Don't hit me!

Slinger flips rapidly in the sky, narrowly avoiding Gold-bug. With one quick turn, he soars towards his now-falling teammate and grabs him before he hits the ground.

Gold-bug: Sorry man! I lost control.

Slinger: Don't worry about it. I'm going to drop you in that tank. Once you're in there... Well... You know what to do.

Gold-bug: Um... What do I do?

Slinger: Are you serious? What do you think?

Slinger lines himself up with the tank below, and carefully calculates where to drop Gold-bug so that he falls directly into the opening at the top.

Gold-bug: Well, I would assume that....

Slinger drops him before he can finish his sentence, causing him to revert back into cannonball mode in order to break his fall.

Valorack soldier: We have an incoming... Well... I don't know what it is, but it's coming in fast!

Suddenly Gold-bug slams into the interior of the tank and remains in ball form.

Valorack soldier: Um... What is it?

Valorack gunman: Should we shoot it?

The two soldiers look at each other without speaking, then both turn almost simultaneously to fire at the armored gold sphere before them.

This continues for quite some time until the men finally notice the bullets bouncing off and into the tank and cease their fire.

Valorack soldier: Look! It's moving!

Gold-bug starts to shake vigorously to confuse the men. In the blink of an eye, he pops out of ball form with both guns aimed at the men and stands upright.

Gold-bug: Bye-bye...

Gold-bug begins to unload both of his guns inside the tank, completely clearing it of men.

Nearby, Steampunk, Contra, and Bucket stand back to back with their weapons trained on Valorack soldiers and ready to fire.

A horde of Valoracks surround the three.

Steampunk: Wait until they're close, then unleash.

Contra: Hey guys... Let's talk about this. Really, I don't want to hurt anybody. It's all okay.

Valorack soldier: Wait... Really?

Contra: Nope...

Contra immediately swings his hammer with crushing force and takes out six soldiers.

Steampunk: I just said to wait... Ughhhh!

Steampunk and Bucket flank Contra and start firing.

They both discharge rounds in a steady stream as Contra continues to slam through gangs of enemies.

Valorack gunman: I'm going to shoot the bucket off of your head!

Steampunk laughs at the comment.

Bucket: Shut up man!

Bucket gets angry and attacks the man who made the comment.

Steampunk activates his shoulder gun and fires at the men behind him, as he shoots forward with his handgun.

Steampunk: Watch the tank!

Steampunk looks over to see an enemy tank approaching.

He activates his jump boost and leaps high in the air.

Bucket: Woah! I didn't know you could do that. Wait... Why can't I do that?

Steampunk lands on the nearby tank and grabs a metal handle hanging off of the side. He activates his chainsaw and begins tearing through the side of the tank. Sparks fly with no visible damage, showing him that his chainsaw isn't strong enough to penetrate the frame.

Suddenly, Gold-bug pops his head out of the top of the tank.

Gold-bug: Stop stop stop stop!

Steampunk looks up at Gold-bug, who is grinning with a sense of accomplishment.

Gold-bug: Are you proud of me? I can't see your face through the mask but I assume you look proud.

Steampunk: How about you aim that tank away from us... Then I'll be proud.

Gold-bug disappears back into the tank and turns it away. Steampunk jumps off and returns to fight next to Contra.

Contra: Should we use bullet storm yet?

Steampunk fires a missile off into the distance.

Steampunk: Not yet... We still need information.

The missile explodes behind him as it makes contact with a nearby tank.

Gold-bug speaks over the COM system.

Gold-bug: You knew that wasn't the tank I was in, right?

Steampunk: One can only hope...

Gold-bug: That's a joke! Heh heh... Funny.

Gold-bug pauses for a moment.

Gold-bug: That is a joke, right?

Steampunk smirks but does not answer.

Nearby, Jazz is preparing to attack.

Many explosions sound around him, bullets scream past his head. In the midst of all the chaos, Jazz walks calmly forward, unfazed by the turmoil, holding nothing but his guitar.

Valorack Commander: What is he doing? These are the strangest people I've ever seen.

Jazz stops moving as a line of men form in front of him. He calmly holds the guitar in his hands, as if he's about to play a song. He looks up to reveal his face as his top hat casts a shadow on his eyes. His long black hair moves in the wind, revealing his face even more.

Valorack soldier: Don't move! Stay right there!

Jazz: Hey, hey... Calm down. It's all okay. Let's just all relax.

The men look confused by Jazz's calm words.

Jazz: Just let me play you a song. What do you guys like? You seem like the bluegrass type.

The men don't respond.

Jazz: Okay... Maybe not so much. You like jazz?

One of the Valorack men starts to raise his hand but quickly lowers it when the soldier next to him notices.

Jazz: I like jazz, in fact... that's my name. You know what though? Today seems like a heavy metal kind of day.

Jazz starts to strum the guitar. A loud, distorted electric guitar noise rushes out from the brass-forged guitar. The chords he plays are basic to start, but then he begins to build louder and louder. The men are completely caught off guard by this and stand in place, almost dropping their weapons in amazement. Jazz suddenly pauses.

Jazz: This is my favorite part!

The front of the neck of the guitar opens up and three very narrow gun barrels slide forward...

Jazz: The solo!

Jazz starts to skillfully play a very intricate guitar solo. As he picks at the strings, bullets fly out of the guitar's barrels in tune with each note. Every chord he strikes sends a burst of lead towards his enemies like the blast of a shotgun.

Spent bullet shells begin to fall out of the base of the guitar.

Valorack commander: Are you kidding me?! I'm losing my men to a guitar?

The whole line of Valorack men fall from the unsuspected firepower. All that remains is the commander.

Jazz: What can I say? I'm so good it killed 'em.

The commander reaches behind him and detaches the axe strapped to his back.

Valorack commander: What can your instrument do against my axe?

He says this with a content grin on his face, certain that he has Jazz beat.

To the commander's surprise, Jazz grabs the guitar by its neck and flips a lever on the side. The sides of the base of the guitar open up to expose two axe-like blades. He holds the guitar against his shoulder showing that the instrument is now in axe.

Valorack commander: Oh come on!

Jazz and the commander charge at each other and the two axes make contact, sending sparks as they connect.

Across the base, Hevy is attempting to take out all of the remaining tanks with the "Barnstormer".

The tanks all seem to be unmanned. None of them are moving.

Hevy: Anyone in there?

All the tanks in perfect synchronization turn their barrels and take aim on Hevy. This either startles him or amuses him – it's quite difficult to tell.

Hevy: Oh my! Don't scare me like that boys. I'm too old for a fright like that.

He soon realizes that he should do less talking and more firing as the tanks prepare to obliterate him.

The barrels on his gun begin to spin as he prepares to fire.

Hevy: Clang... I might need some back up!

He pulls the trigger and a massive tornado of bullets charge forward destroying the tanks in front of him. Missiles explode all around Hevy as he presses forward and fires as much as he can at the remaining tanks.

Slinger: Fall back Hevy! You're going to get yourself killed!

Slinger flies above Hevy as Clang approaches from the side.

Clang: Keep firing, let me charge up the soundwaves.

Hevy: Oh, by all means take your time... I'll just be dodging certain death!

Clang's boots fire spikes down into the ground to stabilize him as he recharges his "bass cannons".

Slinger drops bombs from above onto the tanks below in an attempt to weaken the outer shell.

Clang: Okay... I'm ready.

Clang holds his two gauntlets out and releases huge soundwaves. An earth-shattering bass reverberates out, unleashing wave after wave of sonic destruction.

The entire base turns to the source of the sound as the intense waves deteriorate the line of tanks pursuing them.

Hevy continues to fire the "Barnstormer" at the tanks using the little ammo he has left. Slinger lands and begins to fire as well.

Slinger: Don't let up, Clang!

Clang: What?!

Slinger: I said don't let up!

Clang: Nah man I didn't leave the oven on... Don't worry.

Clang continues to send the soundwaves forward, not being able to hear what Slinger says.

The five tanks stop firing as they finally implode from the endless firepower.

Jazz continues to fight the Valorack Commander nearby. Their axes send loud ringing throughout the camp as the metal weapons strike each other.

The Commander swings and misses Jazz, lodging his axe in the ground below. Jazz takes this moment of vulnerability to strike as he jumps and kicks the man away from the axe.

Jazz: So, now for the question of the day...

Jazz slowly approaches the fallen man.

Jazz: Where is Ronin Torchwood hiding?

The Valorack commander starts to laugh under his breath.

Valorack Commander: Is that what this is all about? You want to find Ronin? Ha Ha Ha HA HA!

Jazz holds his hand up ready to strike the man with his steel tipped fingers. Suddenly, a shard of metal pierces into Jazz's back, causing him to fall to the ground in pain.

Bolts appears on the scene with both lightning whips fully activated.

Bolts: Jazz what happened? Where did that come from?

Jazz: Don't worry about it, just keep fighting.

Bolts gets closer to examine the wound.

Bolts: No dude that's serious. You need to get that fixed soon! You're losing a lot of blood!

Four Valoracks approach them from behind.

Bolts turns around quickly and cracks the lightning whip in his left hand, wrapping in around the legs of one of the men. He retaliates by firing three shots at Bolts. His armor deflects these bullets but suffers significant damage.

Jazz: It's just a piece a shrapnel… I'll… I'll be fine.

Boltz presses a button that energizes the whips even more, electrocuting the man. He quickly releases the whip from the man's legs swinging them around, striking the remaining men.

Bolts: Jazz is down. Someone come help us.

Clang answers over the COM.

Clang: I'm coming!

Bolts: NO… Not you.

Clang: Are you serious? I can help him.

Bolts: Yeah, and that's how our dog died when we were kids.

Clang: Are you ever going to let that go?!

Bolts: NOOOOO! He was too young to die!

Jazz: Meanwhile I'm still bleeding out!

Bucket runs to the scene.

Bucket: Hold still, I've got this.

The fallen Valorack Commander starts to get up when suddenly Steampunk comes up behind him, kicks him to the ground again and places a metal ring around the man. With the press of a button, the ring folds out creating a cage around the man and linking to the ground.

Valorack Commander: What? Let me out of this! I refuse to play these games any longer!

Steampunk: Shhh… shhh… The adults are talking. Stop whining.

The commander looks at Steampunk completely bewildered.

Valorack Commander: Adults? ADULTS? I am an adult! I'm talking!

Steampunk runs to Jazz's aid.

Bucket: It's really in there.

Steampunk: You're going to have to pull it out, Hudson.

Bucket: Why me?

Jazz lays on the ground, still bleeding.

Jazz: Because you're the sanest one here. And that's sad given you have an actual bucket on your head.

A bullet flies in from the distance and hits the bucket on his head. Hudson turns and immediately shoots the man who fired the shot.

Bucket: See… This bucket just saved my life.

Bolts: Where did you get a bulletproof bucket?

Bucket: Not important, what *is* important is Jazz's favorite color.

Jazz looks confused.

Jazz: What does my favorite color have to do with... ARHHHHHH!

Bucket pulls the shrapnel out of Jazz's back mid-sentence, distracting him from the pain. Bucket quickly grabs a bandana hanging from Jazz's belt loop and presses it into the wound to stop the bleeding.

At this moment, everything is silent. All the men in the camp seem to be gone or hidden, so the team regroups with the others.

Gold-bug jumps out of his tank and rolls over to the scene. Slinger lands down from above and deactivates his wings.

Slinger: I think we did it, guys.

Steampunk looks skeptical of the sudden silence and begins walking toward the commander in the cage.

Contra: I could have sworn there were more men when we got here.

Steampunk takes aim at the commander.

Steampunk: Where did Ronin run off to on Judgment Day? I need answers now!

The commander starts to laugh.

Commander: Is that what this is about? Oh, you poor thing. He's gone!

The rest of the team looks at the commander. Hevy and Clang walk over to the cage as well.

Clang: You're lying! Tell us where he is!

Hevy: Trust me bud... You don't want to make him mad.

Commander laughs more at the sight of Clang jumping around angrily.

Steampunk casually shoots the man in the leg.

Commander: Arrghhhh! What are you thinking? I swear on my life he's not on earth! He escaped and went somewhere. We're trying to find him too! Until he comes back we're just, holding things down.

Steampunk: Ugh, how noble of you.

Bolts: Hey man, you might want to see this!

Steampunk: I swear I will stop at nothing to get that diamond back, and if you are in any way trying to keep me from it, you will regret it.

Slinger: Guys turn around!

Contra swings his hammer at the cage causing the commander to fall.

Contra: You don't want to mess with us man! I would suggest answering our question.

Slinger: CHASE!!!!

Steampunk turns around quickly upon hearing this. He is not used to being called by his real name while on the field. The three turn to see a huge fleet of tanks approaching from the distance.

Hevy: Well. Isn't that just... terrifying.

Contra: Bullet storm now?

Steampunk is hesitant to answer.

Steampunk: Yeah, bullet storm.

Contra: Okay. Everyone in formation! Bullet Storm is a go!

Bolts: Are you serious! We've never done that before!

The tanks approach closer and closer as the team forms a line.

Bucket: What's going on!

Steampunk: You all know what to do! Activate now!

The team's guns open and connect to each other in the most intricate ways, as if the metal is almost alive. Jazz slowly stands and joins the team in this action. Hevy's gun opens in the back and connects to Steampunk and Bucket's guns. They all shape-shift and merge to look like one big makeshift weapon of destruction. Clang and Gold-bug place their weapons on the sides, as they break and reconnect to the huge weapon. Slinger's gun connects along the side as well.

Commander: You guys seriously are the most confusing team of people I have ever seen!

Contra places his hammer on top and it opens to reveal a rocket launcher. Jazz places his guitar near the bottom and it latches in, completely changing form.

All the weapons at this point have totally transformed from what they once were, and have merged to create one huge cannon of a weapon.

The tanks seem just a few yards away from the team at this point.

Steampunk: What for my command!

The last piece of the behemoth gun is connected as Bolts attaches his whips to the back, thus powering the weapon.

Jazz: They are getting closer!

Steampunk: Not yet! We only have one shot at this.

Hevy: Steampunk, buddy, we need to fire!

Steampunk: Not Yet!!!!

The tanks begin to take aim as the gunners prepare to fire.

Bolts: I need to do it now!

Clang: Wait!

The team looks at Clang in confusion.

Clang: I think I actually did leave the oven on.

Steampunk: Bolts, now!!!

Bolts activates the whips and the massive titan of a gun fires a huge blast of red energy. All that is seen in front of the men is bright white firepower. The team goes flying back but bolts hangs on with all he can to the back of the gun, keeping the charge active.

The team holds onto anything they can find, trying not to be blown away in the wake of the intense blast.

Contra: Bolts... Hang... on!

Bolts: I can't... fire... much... longer!

The entire left wing of the base is completely engulfed with the blast as it starts to die down. Shell casings fly off the gun in five different constant streams.

Finally, the blast comes to a sudden halt. Bolts lays on the ground completely worn out.

The team slowly gets up to assess the damage.

The tanks have been completely destroyed and all that's left is the scorched earth below, with bits and pieces of shrapnel from the tanks.

The whole team is silent for quite some time.

Clang: Yep, I definitely left the oven on.

Hevy starts to laugh.

Hevy: Haha! That was quite the spectacle.

The canon begins to disconnect and the guns revert back to their original design. They lay on the ground steaming and overheated.

Steampunk walks back over to the commander who is dumfounded. All is silent.

Steampunk: You see what we can do? Now I'm going to ask you one more time…

The Commander struggles to find his voice after witnessing the overwhelming firepower.

Commander: He's not on earth. He just isn't.

Slinger: I think he's telling the truth man.

Steampunk takes off his mask, breathing the fresh air again. He looks very discouraged.

Steampunk: Fine then. Let's move out team.

The team collects their guns and begins to turn and leave the base.

Commander: You're no different than us! You know that!

Steampunk stops in his tracks and turns to the man.

Steampunk: And how is that?

Steampunk gets close to the cage so that he can see the man face to face.

Commander: Look at all the manslaughter you committed. All my men! This whole base massacred!

Steampunk: Think of all the countless lives you've ended! Someone had to stop you!

Commander: We're both fighting for a cause we believe in! We both kill those who get in our way. We're no different... not at all. You think you're right... and I think I'm right.

Steampunk shouts angrily and aims his gun at the caged man's head.

Commander: Go ahead, shoot me! Prove me right!

Steampunk looks down as these words hit him. The words pierce him. He starts to think that the man may be right. Maybe they're not that different.

He drops the gun back down to his side and turns to walk away once more.

Contra: Come on man. Don't let him do that to you.

Steampunk: Let's go! We're done here.

Chase and the team hesitantly walk away, leaving the man in his cage.

Commander: This is a war kid! AND WE WILL WIN THIS WAR!

Steampunk stops walking as he remembers his father's last words to him. He looks down at the bullet on his necklace as the words "Make War," ring clear in his mind.

He quickly turns and fires, causing the other team mates to jump.

Steampunk: We're not the same…

We win wars.

Not you.

———————————————————

The team is now back at their cabin in Fair Grove. This special place is called "Abraham's cabin," and was rebuilt by Chase, Tristen and his uncle Gregory.

All the teammates guns are laying across a table, still hot from battle. Hevy stands by, reloading and working on the guns.

The rest of the team sits at a long wooden table laughing and drinking gallons of barrel-aged ginger ale from Lankford's pub.

Steampunk is no longer armored and stands on the porch outside the house looking at the starry night sky. Slinger (Tristen) walks out to meet him.

Slinger: Hey Chase, your cousin is on the news.

Chase looks at the ground and sighs.

Chase: What did he do this time?

Chase and Tristen walk into the main room to watch the TV. The other members of the team continue to laugh and joke obnoxiously at the table as they drink more ale.

Reporter: "After years of pursuit, Gideon Maverick has finally been brought into custody. Authorities say he will serve a fifty-year sentence for multiple counts of grand theft auto, larceny, breaking and entering, and defacing of public property.

Clang: It's about time they found that kid.

Hevy: Hey man, show some respect! That's his cousin and I was supposed to be responsible for him too, before he ran out and started a rampage of crime those years back.

Chase: It's fine. Me and him had our problems. By the time he ran away we didn't even know each other anymore.

Jazz: He was always a jerk in high school. Still a shame to see what became of him.

Chase starts to answer but notices his phone ringing.

He picks it up to see that his friend and fellow redeemer Teddy McClellan is calling.

Chase: Hey Kore. What's up?

Teddy: Hey man, how'd it go today?

Chase: Not good. I mean we took out a huge portion of the Valorack, but Ronin... and the diamond. Looks like they're not on earth.

Teddy: Dang man. That's no good. After what he did to Dawn, he needs to be pursued.

Chase: I know. How is everyone else. Have you heard from Cody?

Teddy: No, he's still off looking for Silver... I mean Gladstone.

Chase: Why does he still have faith in her? She betrayed us. I'd leave it at that. Rebekah, Silver, Jinx Gladstone, whatever she is. She's a traitor.

Teddy: Well, he has enough faith in her to search and find her. Wrong or not, he's following his heart.

Contra: You know back in the day, they used to call me the snake. Ha ha!

Gold-bug: Why on earth would they call you that?

Contra: Because, you'd never see me coming. Just like a snake bite.

Chase: Hey keep it down! I'm on the phone!

Teddy: Who was that?

Teddy voice reveals concern.

Chase: That was just Contra. He's really loud. Ignore him.

Teddy: Oh okay. His voice sounded familiar… strange. Anyways, what's your next plan?

Chase: I… I honestly don't know. We've got to find the diamond. But if it's not on earth, I don't know where to look.

Teddy: Let us help you man. The diamond is just as much the Redeemers responsibility as it is yours.

Chase: Don't worry about it. You guys focus on…. well. What are you guys focusing on these days?

Teddy: Nothing crazy. Just some basic Orion City crime watch and some Bedrock Arc Stone research.

Chase: Well that's important too. Just stick with that.

Teddy: Oh, by the way. Noah came back to the team today.

Chase: Really? It's been awhile.

Teddy: He brought his brother, too. They're both part of the team now.

Chase: Is he using the Speed Diamond again?

Teddy: He's thinking about it. After all that happened on Judgement Day, he's not too keen on killing again.

Chase notices someone outside the house standing on the porch.

Chase: Hey man I got to go... We'll talk again soon.

Teddy: All right, see you around Steampunk.

Chase opens the glass pane door and walks out onto the porch.

Chase: Well, well, well... What reason have you to be here, of all places?

???: Not happy to see me?

Chase: Well, technically, I don't know who you are.

The man speaking walks out of the shadows. It is none other than The Watcher. This is a man whose persona is unknown. He always wears a black robe and a metal skull mask with bright red eyes.

Watcher: I am happy to see you.

Chase and The Watcher shake hands after not seeing each other for some time. The Watcher helped found the Redeemers with Drake and now leads the team in Drake's absence. Little does Chase know, Drake is still alive and stands before him.

Watcher: I take it today wasn't a success.

Chase: It sure wasn't. Every time I think I'm closer to finding the diamond, it moves farther away.

The two stand silent for a while.

Watcher: Michael attempted to escape through a portal, and we know that Ronin escaped through it as well, right?

Chase: Yes, it's true. But now it looks like that portal didn't lead to anywhere on earth.

Watcher: He could have easily gone to another dimension.

Chase: It just makes no sense to me. We had been warped out. The bomb dropped. He should have been there when it dropped. Next thing you know, he's still alive and has an army working for him. How do you find someone in another dimension when the portal that opened was completely random and could lead anywhere? Where do you look first?

The Watcher starts to answer, when he sees the writing on Chase's armored shoulder. "I fight in memory of Drake and win until Dawn's return." This one piece of armor he leaves on even if he's taken the other armor off.

Watcher: That message on your shoulder. We've... never really talked about what happened. How are you doing?

Chase takes a deep breath before answering.

Chase: I still here his voice. I even see Justin sometimes. It's all in my head though.

Watcher: No one ever sacrificed as much as Justin did.

Chase: But you know what they say, right? Dawn will return.

Watcher: Do you really believe that?

Chase: Well, he wouldn't tell a lie, would he? He said he wasn't capable of telling a lie.

Watcher: That is true...

The Watcher stops mid-sentence and looks at the message on Chase's shoulder once again. This time he focuses on the name Drake.

Watcher: And what about Drake? What does he mean to you?

Chase: Drake gave me the opportunity to be part of a family again. Even though I left the team, I'm still a part of that family. And now I have an "orphan club," of my own to watch out for.

Chase chuckles but The Watcher does not. The Watcher is silent.

Watcher: There is something you don't know about. I've been waiting for the right time to tell you.

Chase looks confused and does not reply.

Watcher: You must promise to tell no one about this. It's life or death.

Chase: Okay, I promise.

The Watcher reaches up to take his mask off revealing the face of Drake.

Chase stumbles back at this sight.

Drake: I know you're probably shaken and don't understand how this is possible...

Chase: You... You shouldn't be here... I... How did this...

Drake starts to answer, but quickly leaves the scene as someone else approaches.

Bucket: Hey, are you okay man? There is something you need to see.

Chase is still in shock and everything around him seems to be in a blur. He can't get a grip on reality after what he just saw.

Chase: Yes, I'm... I'm fine. What is it?

Hudson leads Chase into the living room, where the team stands in a huddle staring at a weird yellow aura forming on the wall. It looks almost like an illuminated gear, turning as it opens up on the wall.

Hevy: Should we throw something at it?

Contra: I say we shoot it.

Chase looks carefully at the spinning yellow circle on the wall, noticing it begin to open up like a portal.

Chase: Everyone back up!

Suddenly the portal opens and four people stand on the other side of it.

A tall man in a brown top hat enters first. He wears a brownish colored jacket that falls down behind him like a tail. In his hand is an intricately designed cane. He has long sideburns that grow out almost to his chin. Moving around his arms are yellow aurora gears of some magical energy. The man speaks up.

???: Hello mates. I hear your looking for a diamond.

Slinger picks up the nearest gun and takes dead aim at the man.

???: Please, no need for violence. My name is Cogsmire, and today, I'll be your guide straight to the Power Diamond. How does that sound?

Chase looks even more confused as the face of the British man before them looks identical to Drake.

Chase: Drake I swear! If you're joking with me right now!

Cogsmire: Oh heavens no! Who is this Drake you speak of?

Slinger: Chase what is going on?

Chase looks completely bewildered, as does the rest of the team.

Chase: Who are you? Why are you here? How can we trust you?

Cogsmire: I already answered that question. My name is Cogsmire, master of the mystic arts. Student under the teaching of Jengo Darkbane himself, and guardian of New Brassport City. Why am I here? Well, to bring you to Ronin of course! And how can you trust me?

Cogsmire removes his hat and holds to his side.

Cogsmire: Chase Williams... I know your father.

Day 1 (Gideon)

Masquerade

1 Day earlier

Gideon and his friend Mathias sit in his red sports car as they watch the people walk into Surge Tower, the energy epicenter of Orion City.

Gideon: So let's run over the plan again.

Gideon speaks in his usual raspy tone as his long black hair covers his eyes.

Mathias: We go in, sneak past security and find Ben Craftian.

Gideon: Yep.

Mathias: Is that really all we're going off of. Just sneak past security and find Ben... The head of Surge Tower... Surge himself.

Gideon: Our intel shows that Ben Craftian has been funding evil corporations. When the Royale was around, its primary source of income was from Surge Ltd. No one has questioned him since - for reasons I don't understand. So... we have to take this chance.

Mathias: Fine, but let me do all the talking. I don't want your angst getting in the way.

Gideon: Of course. I'm way too popular a face to bringing attention to myself.

Mathias: Yeah, one guard sees you and you're done.

Gideon puts his hair into a bun and places his hood on his head.

Gideon: Let's go then.

Gideon and Mathias make their way into the huge entrance of Surge Tower. The main lobby is mainly empty, except for a few men in business suits walking to the elevator.

The two try to get to the elevator, but are stopped by the receptionist.

Receptionist: Excuse me men, do you have an appointment?

Gideon gestures for Mathias to talk.

Mathias: Umm…. Yes. Just with the B wing bureau. We have interviews.

The receptionist looks at the two suspiciously, taking note that they are wearing torn jeans and jackets.

Receptionist: You definitely don't look like you're here for an interview. What's the name?

Gideon begins to type something on his phone as a list of names appears. He clicks on two names and shows them to Mathias.

Mathias looks down at the names: Matthew Johnson and Samuel Evens.

Mathias: Umm… Matthew Johnson and Samuel Evens. Ma'am…

The receptionist looks the names up to see that these men did in fact have an appointment scheduled.

Receptionist: Well, what do you know. You two are scheduled for 2:00 on the third floor.

Mathias: Thank you.

The two leave the desk and make their way to the elevator. A group of men are passing by them and Gideon accidentally bumps into one of them.

Gideon: I am so sorry, sir.

Surge Tower Worker: Please watch where you are going.

Gideon and Mathias enter the otherwise empty elevator.

Mathias: How did you know those names where right?

Gideon: I hacked into their system, found the schedule, and picked two men registered for interviews.

Mathias: Incredible! I was so nervous. But wait, there is a problem. We need a key card to get to the top floor.

Gideon reaches in his pocket and holds up a key card.

Gideon: I picked this up from the worker I bumped into.

Mathias: For real?

Gideon: Yeah, that wasn't an accident.

Gideon presses the button for floor four.

Gideon: There is something I need to see first.

Mathias: What do you mean? We don't need to waste any more time here than we have to.

Gideon: Just follow me.

The elevator door opens and the two exit. They stop at each corner and check before advancing. Finally, they come to one corner and Gideon peeks his head around to see the infamous room 454.

Gideon: There it is. Darren Gresham's old room.

Mathias: Who?

Gideon: Notorious killer. He used to run his operation out of here secretly. No one knew it until a man brought him to justice.

Mathias: Oh yeah, Ryan Martel, right?

Gideon: Yes. I need to see the room. If we're going to prove anything, there is bound to be something in there. I hear they just boarded the place up and never checked it again.

The two make a sprint for the room. They approach the door to see it boarded up.

Mathias: What now?

Gideon roundhouse kicks the planks off the door and opens it.

Mathias: Okay, that's what.

The room is dark and ominous and seems to house a dark energy. The two are silent.

Gideon searches the desk, but finds nothing. All that is left on the desk is a picture of a girl.

Mathias: Why do you think they just locked this place up and never searched it again? I don't understand.

Gideon: That's what I want to know. I feel that whoever runs Surge Tower is part of the organization Gresham was running.

Mathias: Anyone could have just taken the boards down and searched the place. This is really suspicious.

Gideon: What a second... Something isn't right.

Gideon walks slowly to the closet on the right.

Mathias: What are you doing man? I have a bad feeling.

Gideon approaches the door slowly. He grips the handle of the closet door and slowly opens it.

Mathias: Oh my word! Close it man! That is horrible...

Gideon doesn't jump back at all, as he looks into the closet to see two dry skeletons propped against the wall.

He pulls out his phone and takes a picture of the sight.

Gideon: There is our evidence. It's not much but they do owe an explanation.

Mathias: Let's just get out of here.

The two leave the room and make a sprint for the elevator. Luckily no one is around so they walk right in.

Gideon places the key card in the slot and they make their way to the top floor.

Mathias: What about the cameras? Why hasn't anyone seen us?

Gideon: I set the cameras on a delay. Five-minute delay to be exact. We don't have much time.

Mathias: Are you serious?

The door opens and the two exit the elevator. All that lays before them is a wide glass pane. On the other side of the glass is a huge, immaculate office. Sitting in the office is

Ben Craftian, the owner of Surge Ltd., staring out over the cityscape of Orion.

Gideon: There he is. Are you ready to find answers?

Mathias: At this point, we don't have a choice.

Gideon: Good.

The two run at the glass pane. They kick open a door and charge at Ben.

Ben turns quickly to send a blast of electricity at the men from a gauntlet. This sends the two-flying back.

Ben: Hello men, good to see you.

Gideon picks himself off the ground as he looks up to see many computer monitors displaying footage of them approaching the top floor.

Ben: Please, have a seat... What's this all about?

Mathias looks to Gideon, confused. Gideon nods at Mathias and the two sit down in the chairs.

Ben: They call me Surge, you know? Ever since The Redeemer left Orion City, they look to me as their savior.

Gideon: Very fascinating, not relevant though...

Ben: Sure it is. If everyone sees me as their savior, what reason have you to see me as an oppressor.

Mathias: We believe you're hiding something. A double-life, if you will. A kind of, skeleton in the closet.

Ben: And what would that be?

Gideon: The fact that there are actual skeletons in your closet.

Gideon shows Ben the picture of the two skeletons in Gresham's closet.

Gideon: And not just that, but you've been funding a lot of other openly evil organizations.

Mathias: And why has no one been in that room since Gresham died?

Ben: Oh you boys really shouldn't make such a fuss.

These words ring through Gideon's mind.

Gideon: What you just said... those words. I once knew someone who would say that all the time.

Mathias: What are you talking about, Gideon?

Gideon: You're not really Ben Craftian. Are you...

Ben doesn't respond.

Gideon's heart drops in his chest.

Gideon jumps up quickly and kicks Ben in the face with incredible force.

To Mathias's surprise, Ben's face seems to rip clean off and fly across the room.

Ben quickly holds his head in his hands as his "face" falls on the floor.

Mathias: OH MY GOSH!!!

Mathias starts to feel sick as he looks down to see the face digitally turn off, revealing that it was just a white mask, much like one worn for a drama production.

Mathias: You don't mean.

Gideon: It's *Masquerade*.

Mathias and Gideon look up to see a completely faceless man. All that is before them is a pale bald head with a mouth and two X's for eyes cut in with a knife. This horrifying thing standing before them is the evil deceiver Masquerade.

Masquerade: I will be the people's savior, and you will not stop me!

He runs over to the fallen white mask and places it back on his face. It forms back into the shape of Ben Craftian's face.

He then quickly shoots Mathias in the leg and exits the room. The security system locks the door behind him and the two are trapped inside.

Mathias: Gideon, help me!

Gideon: I'm coming man, stay put.

Gideon starts to run over to Mathias, but notices something beeping under the desk.

Gideon: Mathias! Get down now!!!

Suddenly a huge explosion rips through the office and Gideon is thrown out of the building.

He falls rapidly towards to ground.

Gideon: NO! Not like THIS! I'm NOT READY!!!

Gideon closes his eyes.

All goes silent.

He sees within the blackness, two figures. One of them bright and robed in white, one of them dark and dressed with red horns. Behind the two figures are two glowing eyes. One of them red and one of them blue. He hears the two voices say:

"May the powers of the Dark Dwelling and Akarius be with you now, chosen one."

Gideon opens his eyes.

The world around him is foggy as he sees flashing blue and red lights approaching.

He looks around to see that he is on the ground outside of Surge Tower. A crater has formed around him.

Gideon: What!? How did I survive!

Officer: Hands up! Don't move!

Gideon is in shock as to how he feels no pain or took no damage from the fall. The officer handcuffs him and moves him into a nearby police vehicle.

Gideon has been caught. His next stop is prison.

Day 2

New Brassport City

Hevy: How do you know 'em? He's been dead for years. You better start talking!

Cogsmire: Calm down will you! By my festive hat, you mates are quite the boisterous lot, aren't you?

Chase: Honestly, you're the least confusing thing that's happened to me today. Just start talking please. What's the deal?

Cogsmire: Ah yes. I knew ole Abraham in his day. A swell fellow. But that is not important. What is important is..

Slinger: No. no. no... Prove that you knew him.

Cogsmire: I was speaking. So very rude of you to interrupt the great Cogsmire. But alas, I shall comply.

Cogsmire reaches into his pocket to reveal a stopwatch.

Cogsmire: This was...

Chase: My dad's stopwatch. Or at least one of them.

Cogsmire: Again with the interruptions!

Jazz: You walked into our house completely uninvited, I don't want to hear it.

Clang enters the room. No one noticed he was gone until now.

Clang: Guys, I turned the oven off. It's all good... Woah... What happened here?

Cogsmire: Hello there, my name is Cogsmire, master of the mystic...

Clang: Oh, hi there! I'm Clang.

Bolts: No one cares...

Clang: Shut up!

Cogsmire: Oh bother! If anyone interrupts again...

Chase: Why are you here? You've yet to explain.

Cogsmire puts his hat back on his head and breathes deeply, having been interrupted a fourth time.

Cogsmire: I'm here to take you to Brassport to see Ronin Torchwood.

Contra: Brassport? You mean the wasteland outside of Orion City?

Cogsmire laughs joyfully.

Cogsmire: No, no. You fool!

Contra: I'm sorry. What?

Cogsmire: Oh do calm down, G.I. Joe. The real Brassport - New Brassport City. Finest establishment in the Industrial Dimension.

Bucket: The Industrial Dimension?

Cogsmire: Oh you've got to be... Actually, I take that back, seeing that you have a bucket on your head, I shouldn't expect too much intelligence from you.

Hudson, rather embarrassed, takes the bucket off of his head.

Hudson: At this point I'd rather have my head blown off than hear another joke about the bucket.

Slinger: It's still your name though. Ha ha.

Chase: How do you know we're looking for Ronin?

Cogsmire: Well, I should assume that you two are best friends, given how often he speaks of you.

Hevy: You hear from him? Do you work for him?!

Cogsmire: No, no! Heavens no! That man has gone mad. I'd never spend my time with a basket case like that. But, unfortunately, he makes his home at New Brassport and just will not stop rambling about Chase Williams.

Chase looks startled. He's still wrestling with the fact that Drake is still alive and that this man standing before him looks just like Drake.

Cogsmire: So... Shall we go. I can't keep this portal open forever.

Bolts: You mean that portal just leads straight to New Brassport.

Cogsmire: Why yes. So... Do we have a plan?

He holds the stopwatch out as an offering to Chase. Chase does not take it, but agrees to enter the portal.

Chase: Suit up men. It's time to find Ronin.

Hevy: You'd better not be lying.

Jazz: Yeah, you don't want to be on our bad side.

Cogsmire: Or what? You'll hit me with your guitar?

Jazz activates his guitar into axe-mode.

Jazz: Yeah, maybe I will.

Cogsmire snaps his fingers and the axe disappears from sight and reappears in Cogsmire's hands.

Jazz looks at him angrily. Cogsmire chuckles and hands the guitar-axe back to him.

Chase is fully armored again in his Steampunk attire and the rest of the team follows with their reloaded weapons.

The team stands armed and ready before the portal.

Cogsmire: Very good. Shall we go then? Follow me.

The Guns of Abraham enter the portal after Cogsmire.

Bolts: I don't have a good feeling about this...

Bucket: I trust Steampunk's judgment.

As they enter the portal, gravity seems to shift. They feel a huge weight bear down for a moment as they pass through the dimensional tear between both worlds.

Contra is the last to enter the portal. It quickly closes behind them.

The team looks around to see that they are in a dark hallway. On the walls are paintings of different Industrial Age people. There are three other people waiting for them as they walk down the hallway.

Cogsmire: Allow me to introduce you to some friends of mine who will be assisting us today. This lizard creature is Triggermate. This small man is Drozer. And this fine gentleman here is Gridd. Gridd isn't from here.

Steampunk looks up to see a lizard-like creature standing like a man in brass armor that covers him like scales. On his back is a long sniper rifle.

Triggermate: Hello. I am be nice to meet of you.

Slinger: Um... What?

Cogsmire: He doesn't do words very well but he's still a lovable bloke none-the-less.

Triggermate: I is am very lovable.

A long, spiked tongue protrudes from the lizard man's mouth.

Drozer is a small tan-skinned man who stands about 3 feet in stature. His armor is silver colored and protrudes off of his arms and head. The three main pieces of armor seem to be able to connect and form the spiral pattern of a core-drill bit.

Drozer: Nice to meet you, men.

Gridd is yet another Drake look-alike, and wears a green plaid button up shirt with a hood and blue jeans. His hair is short and spiked in the front. The unique thing about his hair is that it is naturally silver. On his arms he wears stone-laced bracelets that somehow illuminate. Chase notices that there is now a third Drake look-alike before him.

Steampunk: Okay stop! What is going on here! Why do both of you look like Drake Barrows.

Gridd: What is he talking about?

Cogsmire: I'm not quite sure. He keeps rambling on about this *Drake* person.

Hevy: Are you okay, son?

Steampunk: No, I'm not. Today is not a good day.

Gridd walks over to Steampunk.

Gridd: Listen man, I'm not this *Drake* guy.

Gold-bug: You and Cogsmire do look a lot alike though. The only difference is he has sideburns and your hair is silver.

Cogsmire: I don't see the resemblance... Sorry.

Gridd: Thank goodness. I'd hate to look like him.

The Guns of Abraham look at each other, confused, not understanding how they can't see the resemblance.

Triggermate: Gridd and Cogsmire is being my friends.

Gridd: That's right buddy, and we're your friends too, Steampunk. Don't worry about a thing.

Clang: How do you know his name?

Drozer: We've done our research, man.

Bolts: That's creepy. Steampunk you cool with that? He practically admitted to stalking you.

Chase: I'm used to it...

Gridd: The Power Diamond is just as much my business as it is yours. We're on the same team.

Slinger: Why is it important to you?

Gridd turns to look at Slinger.

Gridd: I'm from a space colony called Jettahawk. It's in another dimension. The Power Diamond once vitalized our colony, until the Royale stole it from us a few years back. Now we run off of stored energy and the rest comes from our people who have to slave away almost every day to keep the colony running.

Jazz: So is the diamond still with Ronin?

Cogsmire: That's what we believe. But, he's pretty protected. That's why we need your help. We can't take his army alone, I'm afraid.

Bucket: I see...

Steampunk: Well, were going to get the diamond back, Gridd. Then you can return it back to your colony.

Gridd looks at Steampunk and smiles.

Gridd: Thank you, friend.

The group of 13 come to the end of the hallway to see a huge, circular, deadbolted door.

Cogsmire: Are you ready to see the steam-powered majesty that is New Brassport City.

Contra: You sure we won't bring any unwanted attention to ourselves with the guns and armor and all.

Drozer: Ha ha! I wouldn't worry about that. You guys are going to fit in more than you think.

The yellow gears of magic energy start to glow and intensify around Cogsmire's arms as he holds his right hand in the air and his left hand directly below. The circular door in front of them glows yellow around the edges as well. Cogsmire turns his hands in a clockwise pattern as the ticking of a clock sounds out through the hallway. As he turns his hands, the gears and cogs within the door turn and spin in concert, unlocking the door. As his hands make the final movements, completing one full clockwise turn. The door opens and unveils the city.

Hevy: Amazing!

Gold-bug: I... I can't believe this!

Triggermate: I is at home...

Cogsmire: I present to you all the Industrial Empire of New Brassport City.

The men look around to see tall futuristic bronze metal buildings. Steam billows into the sky forming huge clouds. All around are big gears and pumps turning the steam throughout the city and moving everything around like clockwork. Big brass trains move across tracks carrying people everywhere. The people of Brassport dress similarly to the Guns of Abraham, primarily wearing brass-colored clothing and metal framework accessories. The city and people look very futuristic but also appear to be rustic and modest, as if it were the 1700's. Shops and stores thrive as people buzz in and out. The entire city is well lit by wireframe incandescent lights hanging from poles. Mixed within the crowds of people walking are the occasional robotic humanoids. These figures walk among the humans and seem to go unnoticed. This is strange to Chase, but seems to be fairly similar in appearance to the locals.

Chase: This is truly beautiful.

Gold-bug: And here I was thinking our brass style was unique.

Cogsmire: Oh, no no... That was from us. We did it first.

The men stand still in awe of the city they didn't even know existed.

Cogsmire: Well, let's not dally. Follow me. You see that red light beaming in the air. That's where Torchwood is.

The men start to follow Cogsmire, but realize that there is an immediate drop-off right where they stand.

Contra: How are we supposed to follow you? There is a cliff here.

Cogsmire runs off the edge of the cliff. He starts to fall, but quickly creates a gear-shaped platform of energy below his feet. He begins to jump downward as these platforms form strategically below his feet as if he were running down a set of invisible stairs. He finally approaches the other side of the crevasse and calls up to the others.

Cogsmire: All right then lads, it's your turn!

Drozer and Triggermate run down as Cogsmire creates platforms for them. Gridd reaches behind him and grabs an octagonal capsule on his back. He presses a button on the capsule and it opens, transforming into a hover board. The board glistens a rainbow of colors as it appears to be made of an intricate crystal.

Hevy: What is that thing?

Gridd: This is my Babylon board. It's called the Day-Tracer.

Gridd unbuttons his green flannel shirt and places yellow tinted goggles over his eyes. The bands around his arms begin to glow as the gravity around him and the board charges and focuses into one place. This movement of gravity pushes the other men around and knocks some of them down onto the ground.

Gridd releases this blast and him and the board go flying across the crevasse. He maneuvers and flips himself through the air as he approaches the ground and lands with ease.

From below, he deactivates his board and it reverts to capsule form. He returns the capsule to his back.

Steampunk: Well, I guess it's our turn then.

Bolts: You really just going to trust him?

Jazz: Yeah, why not?

Jazz, being his regular calm self, follows after them jumping on the platforms made for him by Cogsmire.

The rest of the team runs down the gap shortly after. Hevy has the most trouble as he fumbles down the platforms clumsily.

The team finally makes it across the canyon, and they make their way into the main part of the city.

As they walk through the crowd of people, the locals stare and point at Steampunk. The place is filled with an obnoxious murmur as they whisper to each other.

Slinger: Hey man, it looks like your pretty popular around here.

Triggermate: Steampunk is having fame with Brassport peoples.

Steampunk: Hey Cog... What's the deal.

Cogsmire: Well don't you know? You're pretty famous around here, sir!

Gold-bug: How so?

Drozer looks up at Cogsmire with a smirk.

Drozer: Cogsmire, I really don't think they know.

Cogsmire: Well, look ahead! You'll see why they're looking at you.

Steampunk turns around the corner, he has yet to put his mask on, but with the overwhelming number of people looking at him, he considers it. He turns the corner to see a tall metal statue.

Steampunk: I don't understand? What is it?

Drozer: Look closer...

Steampunk walks closer to the statue and reads the name at the base of it.

"Abraham Williams, Our City's Founder"

Steampunk takes a step back to looks up and see a statue of his father towering high.

Hevy: Well, this just baffles me to the gallows and back.

Slinger: Your old man? The Abraham who took me home from school all the time? How?

Steampunk doesn't answer. At this point he is convinced that he is dreaming. After seeing Drake, then two more "Drakes", and now seeing that his father built and founded a city in another dimension, completely bewilders him. Tears begin to fill his eyes.

Triggermate: Oh no... Steampunk is having a sad.

Cogsmire: Listen lad, I know you're confused and..

Steampunk snaps back at Cogsmire.

Steampunk: NO! What is this! I'm tired of not having answers. How is Drake alive? Why do you two both look like Drake? And how the heck did my dad build a city when HE'S DEAD?

Everyone around starts to back up. The team looks very concerned.

Hevy: Chase... Put the gun down.

Chase looks down not realizing he has his gun aimed at Cogsmire.

He hears a familiar voice whisper in his head.

"I feel your pain... I can take it away... just breathe... I'll return soon and fix everything."

Chase places his gun on the ground and falls to his knees.

Steampunk: Explain...

Cogsmire and Triggermate approach Steampunk and place their hands on him. The rest of the team sits beside him in front of the statue.

They all gather around him.

Gold-bug: We're a family Chase.

Bucket: Yeah, whatever this unknown world holds, we're going to go through together, okay?

Jazz plays a tune on his guitar as the crowd of people turn away.

Cogsmire: Your father was born and raised in this dimension. This city was... Well, it didn't exist. But your father had a vision and he saw it through. He built this city and innovatively made it run from steam. Hence the industrial culture.

Gridd: But something happened. The Power Diamond was stolen from this dimension and placed on earth by The Royale. Abraham made it his personal responsibility to get it back. He found it and kept it on earth. He started a new life in Fair Grove and had a child.

Cogsmire: He bragged and bragged about his wonderful boy, Chase. He loved his new life and couldn't see a reason to come back here, so he put me in charge. And I've ruled these people benevolently ever since. And what lovely people they are.

Hevy interjects.

Hevy: So the man who married my sister founded all of this? Amazin'!

Cogsmire: He sure did. He kept the diamond safe to the best of his ability. But... One day, The Royale got it back.

Steampunk breathes deeply.

Steampunk: So that's what happened then... The day he died. The Power Diamond was with him and they killed him to get it back.

Cogsmire is hesitant to answer.

Cogsmire: Yes, but I can see you sought after justice. That mask of their killer lays right there at your side, does it not?

Steampunk looks at the mask. He remembers the reason he fights.

Steampunk whispers to himself.

Steampunk: Redemption... I fight for redemption.

The same voice whispers in his head again.

"Never forget that... I died healing my enemy... Fight with compassion... Fight with healing in mind."

Steampunk regains his composure.

Steampunk: Take me to Torchwood.

The team looks up at him, surprised that he is so ready to fight after having a breakdown only moments before.

Steampunk: I fight for Redemption. I fight to right all wrongs and that's why I'm here. Yes, this is unbelievable and I am hurting.

He pauses and struggles to get the words out.

Steampunk: I am definitely hurting...

But if I choose to give up now... then evil wins. I can't let that happen.

Cogsmire starts to clap and cheer.

Cogsmire: Good show! Truly capital, mate!

Steampunk: Guns of Abraham! It's time we wreak havoc on Ronin Torchwood!

The Guns of Abraham cheer and the entire statue commonplace erupts in cheers as the passersby clap vigorously.

Contra: We're your family... And we're going to fight as one by your side.

Jazz: Yeah man, I'm with you till the end.

Steampunk looks around at his brothers, and remembers the first time he felt a family connection with The Redeemers. He smiles as he turns to look at the red beam shooting into the sky. He places his mask over his head and, with a look of determination, says...

Steampunk: Let's go shoot us a Ronin Torchwood.

Cogsmire: He's up at your father's old mansion. The place is heavily secured by his army, so we can't just waltz on in.

A nearby train stops and the doors open.

Cogsmire: And look, our train is here right on time. Follow me mates.

The team, holding their weapons close, enters the train.

As they enter, each of them takes a seat. Steampunk goes to sit down, but notices someone at the front of the train who looks eerily familiar.

At the front of the train is man in a brown robe. At his sides are two swords with red markings all throughout them. Chase is puzzled at the sight of these swords. They look strangely familiar. The mysterious man turns to reveal a golden skull mask with carvings and artistic etchings all throughout it. Chase takes a seat, but is not content with what he is seeing. He thinks to himself...

"Why does this man look like The Watcher?"

Cogsmire: Everyone, I'd like to introduce you to a friend of mine. He'll be telling us our battle plan today. Everyone, give your attention to The Watcher of Brassport.

Bolts: What are you supposed to be? Why can't we see your face?

Clang: Because he's wearing a mask, idiot.

Contra: What's your name?

Watcher of B: I can't tell you that... I'm sorry. I am on your side. Trust me.

Bucket: How can we know that?

Slinger whispers to Steampunk

Slinger: What's your read on this guy?

Steampunk answers out loud.

Steampunk: You can trust him. I know his type.

The Guns look at each other, perplexed.

Gold-bug: Well, that's awfully racist.

Steampunk chuckles at this comment.

Steampunk: You know what I mean.

Watcher of B: Let me say: it's an honor to see you all.

He looks suspiciously at Steampunk as he says this.

Steampunk gets a weird chill as he looks into The Watcher of Brassport's eyes.

Watcher of B: This train is leading us straight to Abraham's mansion. That is where Ronin Torchwood and the diamond are. Once there, his Psychonauts will attack in droves.

Steampunk: Like Alloys?

Watcher of B: Yes... like... um... Anyway...

The Watcher continues to speak as Slinger whispers to Steampunk

Slinger: What's an Alloy?

Steampunk: The training robots me and the other Redeemers fought.

Slinger: How would he know what that is?

Steampunk: I don't know, I was testing him. Those swords... Those are The Redeemer's swords.

Slinger: Really? How would he have them?

Steampunk: I'm not sure... But I'm going to find out. All of this Drake stuff is confusing me. I need answers.

The two stop talking and listen to The Watcher of Brassport.

Watcher of B: If we can find a way to destroy the majority of his forces and make it to the roof of the house, we should be able to take him down.

Contra: We can do that easily.

Heavy: And have a good time doing it, too.

Drozer: That's what I like to hear! Ha ha!

Gridd: I like these guys.

Triggermate: I has a guns!

Cogsmire: Yes, you do Triggermate. Good boy.

Triggermate strikes a smile from ear to ear across his reptilian face.

Jazz: Looks like we're almost there, guys.

Out of the window is a tall metal mansion surrounded by a tall wall.

The train comes to a stop and the doors open.

Watcher of B: Are we ready, men?

Steampunk looks around at the fourteen men in the train. This is the biggest team he has ever fought with.

Gold-bug: Let's goooooo!

The team gathers their weapons and exit the train.

The train leaves and the large group stands at the base of this towering wall that surrounds the mansion. They look up to see lightning striking in the clouds above and a red beam, soaring endlessly like a laser into the sky.

Drozer without hesitation connects his three pieces of armor together forming a massive drill bit. His armor begins to spin as he jumps into the air and drills into the ground swiftly. He disappears like a mole scurrying away in a garden.

Bolts: Well, he's gone.

Gridd: So um... How do we get over this wall?

Cogsmire walks to the base of the wall.

Cogsmire: It's quite simple really, we just... walk up.

Cogsmire miraculously starts walking up the side of the wall, completely perpendicular to the ground. The team stands back in shock.

Gridd: Oh yeah. You can do that...

Cogsmire: Don't worry guys... I'll get to the other side, then blast you in.

Triggermate: Bye Cogsmortemer!

Triggermate is content and happy as his long lizard tail wags even though he completely mispronounced Cogsmire's name.

Contra holds his warhammer on his shoulder as Cogsmire continues to casually walk up the side of the wall.

Contra: So, where did he learn to make portals and stuff?

Gridd: He studied in the Master Realm for years under the Magi School headmaster, Jengo Darkbane. He studied the ancient technique of trapping monsters in dimensional mirrors.

Steampunk: What kind of monsters?

Gridd: The Hakken... The Brokerra... The Shakterra...

Steampunk's full attention is given to Gridd as he says the name "Shakterra."

Gridd: He learned to harness the power of dimensional mirrors and open them wherever he wants.

Hevy: You sure know a lot about him.

Gridd: Well, I spent a lot of time with him looking for the diamond.

Watcher of B: We are closer than ever now.

Cogsmire has now made it to the other side of the wall. He calls over to Gridd.

Cogsmire: Okay Gridd! I'm going to have to get you to use a gravity blast on the wall at the precise moment I strike it. Sound, well... smashing?

Gridd: Okay! You count down.

Gridd charges up a blast of gravity. He floats in the air slightly as the he focuses gravity in a charged ball between his hands. The stone bands around his arms glow brightly.

Cogsmire: 3... 2... 1!

Gridd releases this blast at the same time Cogsmire releases a blast of energy. As a result, a huge portion of the wall explodes. On the other side of this opening is Cogsmire and Drozer, waiting patiently.

Cogsmire: All right then. Shall we go?

The team walks through the opening in the wall, as a loud, crazed voice emits from a loud speaker.

Ronin Torchwood: Helllooooo travelers! Ha ha ha ha.

The sounds blaring from the speakers are filled with glitches and high pitched noises distorting what Torchwood says.

Steampunk feels a heavy distress fill his body, as he hears the voice of Dawn's killer fill the air.

Torchwood: I've beEN waitinG for a while, Chase! Don't keep me WaitiNg any longer!

Slinger: He's lost his mind, hasn't he!

Steampunk: He definitely sounds a lot crazier than I remember.

Cogsmire: Oh yeah... You should hear him go on and on about you. He's been ranting for you to come fight him for weeks.

Steampunk: Why just me?

Watcher of B: Guys, we have company.

The Watcher of Brassport holds his hands at his sides as they surprisingly ignite into flames. A large horde of Psychonauts pours out of the house and crawls into the stormy exterior.

Torchwood: hahHAHAHAHhahahHAhHAHAHAHAHAHAHHhahahHAHAH! Time to fight, booooys!

The group of 14 stand in a line and prepare to fight off the legion of soldiers as they approach from all angles.

Steampunk's shoulder gun starts to spin. Bucket aims and readies his gun. Clang charges up his soundwave gauntlets. Bolts activates his lightning whips. Contra holds his hammer, ready to smash. Jazz moves his guitar to gun mode. Gold-bug goes into ball form and charges his spin up. Slinger activates his wings and readies his guns. Hevy's "Barnstormer," spins and heats up. Cogsmire creates gears of energy around his arms and the ground around him shines a big yellow gear at his feet. Triggermate moves the sniper gun from his back and smiles big as excitement fills his eyes. The drills on Drozer's hands spin vigorously, and Gridd activates his Babylon board, preparing to glide through the enemies.

Bucket: I really wish I had my bucket right now...

Steampunk: FIRE!!!

Bullets, Magic, Gravity Blasts, Fire, and chaos emits everywhere as the team attacks with force.

Gold-bug and Gridd speed ahead throughout the enemies and knock as many out as they can. Gridd uses the gravity bands around his arms to push a group of Psychonauts together in the air. He slams the clump into the ground and to his surprise, they break and explode into pieces.

Gold-bug slams and ricochets off of enemies and pops out of ball form long enough to shoot a few Psychonauts before going back into ball form.

Gold-bug: Are these guys... Robots?

Gridd turns fast in the air and glides through his foes like a hot knife through butter.

Gridd: It sure looks like it!

Watcher of B: They're not soldiers...

The Watcher releases a billow of fire, destroying a hoard of foes. One of the heads of the mechanical Psychonauts lands in his hand. To his horror, it's the face of a mannequin with scribbled writing all over it. Words like "May you feel that no longer," and "Angel boy healed me???".

He throws the head down and releases quick blasts of fire at each of the approaching foes.

Drozer jumps in and out of the ground like a dolphin jumps through the water as he drills through the layers with ease. Jazz shoots nearby.

He plays chords on his guitar as fast as he can, sending a spray of bullets at the approaching enemies.

Jazz: They're mannequins! Crazed attack mannequins! This is a horror movie turned reality.

Jazz turns his guitar to axe form and breaks into the attackers one after another. Contra jumps in next to him and slams his hammer down on a group of foes.

Contra: This guy has lost his mind! What are these things! They don't even have weapons, they just run around in hordes trying to tackle us. It's horrifying.

Hevy, Steampunk, and Slinger stand side by side, firing waves of bullets.

Hevy's "Barnstormer," completely obliterates waves and waves of the creatures.

Steampunk: Slinger, get to the sky, see where the source of these things is.

Slinger soars upward.

Slinger: On it!

Steampunk and Bucket stand back to back and fire constantly at the mannequins, crawling on the ground.

Bucket: They're dropping like flies, but they just don't stop coming... I don't understand.

Steampunk: There is another motive at play here.

Steampunk flips over Bucket and launches a missile into the sky.

Steampunk: I'm not sure what it is yet.

Cogsmire stands in the middle of the field with a yellow force field around him.

Cogsmire: Well... This is most unprofessional. You're all attacking like mad men!

He releases the force field and immediately fires off blasts of energy from his hands. They each blow through the attackers. He opens countless portals on the ground and the mannequins fall in and enter some unknown realm.

Cogsmire: I'm giving them to you now!

Cogsmire holds his hands in the same 12 and 6 pattern he did when opening the door. This causes a group of enemies to freeze in place. He then, with one swift motion, throws them at Contra. Contra turns to swing his hammer, knocking the horde into a nearby portal.

Cogsmire: Jolly good mate!

Contra: Where are they going?

Cogsmire: Well let's see… Either the Sahara Dessert or Atlantic Ocean. The portals are fairly random though, so who can say. Ho ho!

Cogsmire extends his cane and adds his magic to it to make it a bright whip of energy. Sparks fly off of it as the cane extends and turns into a whip. He throws it forward striking the attackers to the ground while firing energy with his other hand.

Triggermate and Clang run up next to him for support.

Triggermate: I is wanting shoot these spookies.

Clang: Then do it man… thing… Whatever you are!

Triggermate grabs the front of his sniper rifle and pulls it forward, splitting it into two separate rifles. He begins to laugh hysterically as he fires rapidly at the frantic oppressors.

Clang releases his charge of soundwaves from his gauntlets, and the waves break, dismantling the Psychonauts.

Slinger flies overhead and rains down firepower on many of the Pysconaut mannequins that Clang misses.

He makes a full aerial circle, and flies inches from the ground below, firing bullets from barrels that form at the top of his wings.

Gold-bug stands near Gridd and Bolts as they both charge up. Gridd charges up gravity shots and Bolts gets ready to whip enemies. Cogsmire jumps overhead and whips enemies down below with his cane as he jumps on the platforms forming below his feet.

Gridd releases his gravity blasts, sending groups of enemies flying. He then gets back on his Babylon board and soars ahead. As he carves through the air, the enemies get caught in a vortex behind the board, dragging along helplessly behind him.

Bolts strikes his whips strategically at the enemies, knocking them to the ground as Gold-bug slams into the remaining ones.

Hevy stands next to The Watcher of Brassport, as he readies his two swords. The swords fill with fire and Hevy revs up his gun.

Watcher of B: I'll take out any that get too close.

Hevy: I'll shoot the ones far away.

Hevy unleashes the "Barnstormer," on groups of far-away mannequins as The Watcher of Brassport slices through nearby enemies with his flaming swords.

Five mannequins jump onto The Watchers back and tackle him to the ground. Slinger soars by and shoots them off, freeing him. He jumps up and quickly retaliates by sending billows of flames forward as bullets from other teammates continue to soar in all directions.

Torchwood: How DOooo YoOU like my nEW and improved Psychonauts? HAaahhAAAHahaAAahahA!

More and more mannequins pour out of the house.

Slinger: All right I've had enough! I'm going in.

Bucket: We'll back you up! Cogsmire, follow us!

Bucket and Cogsmire follow after Slinger as he flies into the mansion to find the source of the growing number of attackers.

Cogsmire blasts open the door and they both stop to see that the entire interior of the house is covered with crawling mannequins. Their hands and limbs fumble around as they pour out of the house in a frenzy. Slinger immediately turns around as he realizes how outnumbered he is.

Cogsmire: It appears they are all pouring out of some portal in the middle of the house!

Suddenly, the whole front of the house breaks open and thousands upon thousands of hive-minded Psychonauts flood out like a legion of spiders.

Bucket tries to shoot as many as he can, but his attempts are in vain as they completely trample him. Cogsmire opens a portal in front of him to try and collect all the oncoming attackers, but even the portal is overtaken and he is trampled as well.

Steampunk: Guns of Abraham! Form a line! We have to take them down.

The remaining members form a line quickly and attack with all they have left.

Contra shoots a missile out of the handle of his hammer. Jazz shoots as many as he can before having to reload. Drozer stands firm while in drill mode as the creatures run into his drill bit and fall to the side. Gridd holds as many as he can in a gravity hold, while The Watcher of Brassport sends waves of fire forward. Steampunk fires both guns rapidly and activates his chainsaw for the ones that get too close. Clang fires off explosive disks while also sending destructive soundwaves forward. Bolts flings his lightning whips around in a frenzy. Hevy relentlessly unloads the "Barnstormer," while Slinger holds his wings in front of him for protection and also fires his guns. Triggermate stands on Hevy's shoulders towering high above the massive rush of enemies in an attempt to snipe them from above. Goldbug stays in cannonball form as not to be moved.

Slinger: I don't think we can hold them... back!

Steampunk: Don't give... up!

Drozer: They are overtaking us!

Triggermate: I is going to death!

Hevy: AARRRRRRRHHHHHH!!!

The team is overtaken by the mass of mannequins.

All is silent.

The entire ground is covered with lifeless Pysconaut bodies.

Suddenly, the figures start to move like waves in the ocean. The Guns of Abraham, as well as Gridd, Triggermate, Drozer, and Cogsmire are moved to the surface.

Bucket: What's going on? I thought I was dead!

Steampunk: Hudson, don't move! We'll just sink back down.

The men start to move towards each other as the mannequins crowd surf them into one collected pool.

Jazz: Hurry! Everyone grab onto each other.

Each member links arms as they are moved into the middle. The mannequins run around in opposite directions from each other while the team is held up in the middle. Their limbs move and bend in unrealistic ways. Their heads contort in neck breaking manners as they run around in big circles.

Clang: I can't shoot them! I'm out.

Contra: So am I!

Steampunk still has a few bullets left but is too shocked by what is happening to use them. Cogsmire opens a portal on the ground and one of the lines of enemies running in a circle falls into it, one after another. The portal quickly closes as his energy is depleted quickly. New enemies fill in place where the other ones fell.

Cogsmire: This... This is madness! Look at them! It's like some sort of ritual.

Gridd: And we're in the middle of it!

Watcher of B: How do we stop it?

Suddenly all the mannequins stop running. They all stop so abruptly and in place. All falls eerily quiet as their heads turn swiftly to face the men, still held up in the epicenter of the circle.

Torchwood: MoSt ExceLLENt Show!!! HAaaHahaaahaaahHAHAaAHa!

But now... It is time to Face ME!

The Psychonauts start to hoard into the middle where the men are and build onto each other, lifting the men in the air. They climb on top of each other more and more, scaling the group upwards, higher and higher.

Gold-bug: Okay what?! Someone stop this!

Steampunk looks down to see the ground moving farther and farther away as they approach the top of the house where Ronin is. He looks to see the red beam shining up into the sky from the roof of the house, approaching them as they move up.

Steampunk: Get ready men! This is where we get the diamond back.

Gridd: At long last!

The mannequins tilt over and drop everyone into a large opening in the roof of the house. Slinger takes to the sky in order to break his fall. The rest fall quickly into the attic of the house, where Ronin Torchwood stands waiting.

Steampunk and the others hit the ground hard. He regains his composure and looks up to see a horrifying sight. All around the attic are carvings and drawings of Dawn, the redeemer that Ronin killed. Written in red paint are thousands of phrases. They read-

"I killed him."

"He healed me."

"Why did Angel Boy heal me?"

"Dawn of New Death"

"Sky World's fallen angel"

In the middle of the room is the red Power Diamond for which the team has searched all these months. It stays connected to a metal framework that seems to be draining the power from it and shooting it into the sky. Ronin Torchwood moves frantically around the room. Steampunk stands to confront him.

Steampunk: Ronin Torchwood... Your last day has come.

Ronin Torchwood: Has it though? I could have sworn that was scheduled for tomorrow. HaaahahHAHAHahahHAHA!

Ronin has since lost his mind. He appears to have portions of his long spikey blonde hair torn out. His white armored trench coat is torn and withered. On his back is his trademark emerald sword. His eyes are very withered and red.

Gridd: That diamond belongs to me and my people! Hand it over!

Suddenly, the diamond completely vanishes as the last bit of it shoots into the air and the red beam fades.

Torchwood: What diamond?

Gridd, now furious, throws a nearby chair at Ronin. The team charges at him, but stops short when Ronin reveals a metal box with a button on it.

Torchwood: I wouldn't do that if I was you. Otherwise this lovely mansion here will be blown away. _{Hahaha}hahahahaHAHAHAHAHAHAH!

In fact, this whole city will be!

Cogsmire: Oh, you wouldn't dare!

Torchwood: Oh, I *would* though. I really, really *would*.

Steampunk doesn't move as he thinks of a plan to stop Torchwood.

Watcher of B: Where did you take the diamond?

Hevy: We're going to need answers really soon!

Clang: It's been a really bad day trying to find you.

Torchwood grabs a nearby bottle and smashes it on the ground.

Torchwood: CALM DOWN! All will be revealed soon.

Now I know what you're thinking:

How did I end up here?

Why mannequins?

And for goodness sake why did Dawn heal me when I so brutally murdered him!?

Steampunk stares into the eyes of his friend's killer.

Steampunk: Yeah, start talking.

Torchwood grabs a nearby brush and writes on the wall in big letters:

I DON'T KNOW!

Torchwood: I haven't the slightest clue! I've been cooped up here with this diamond just rattling my brain to mush trying to understand why that boy would think to heal me of MY pain when I HAD LITTERALLY STABBED HIM WITH MY SWORD!

He throws his emerald sword at the group and Cogsmire manages to stop it in mid-air before it hits anyone.

Torchwood: That diamond has given me so much knowledge. Seriously you wouldn't believe the stuff I know.

Torchwood pauses for a moment as he shakes his head painfully fast.

Torchwood: Would you believe that we're not even real?

The men look at each other with fear in their eyes. They knew Ronin was crazy but they never knew he was this crazy.

Torchwood: Oh shut up! I'm not that crazy!

The men look around at what or who he could be talking to, but are confused, as it appears he is yelling at the sky.

Torchwood: I'm talking to you, idiot?

...the team looks even more confused.

Torchwood: Oh fine... I'll play your game. It's true gentlemen. We're not even real. We're all just characters in a book. HAHAHAha! I know, right?! It's kind of funny when you think about it.

Watcher of B: You're mad!

Torchwood: No I'm actually not. HAhaahhhahHAhahah! That's what's so funny. Right now, this very moment, we stand in the middle of a book. Nothing we do is up to us, it's all up to what the author chooses. HAaaahaHAHHAHaha! WE HAVE ABSOLUETLEY NO CONTROL!

Bucket targets Ronin, ready to shoot. Steampunk stops him.

Steampunk: Not yet, we still need information.

Torchwood: If you think about it, I didn't even really kill Dawn! The author made me!

Um... How do you know that?

Torchwood: I know everything now *Seth*. That's right... You're not safe anymore.

But... You're just a character. I made you!

Drozer: Who are you taking too!

Torchwood: Oh you can't hear him or see him... But I see him. And he just won't... stop... talking!

Contra: Listen, I'd love to sit here and listen to you talk to yourself and ramble on about us existing in a book or whatever you said, but we need that diamond, and you're going to tell us where it is.

Torchwood: Oh you see, I've read the book start to finish. I know how this ends.

HAHHahahahahahahaHAHHAHAHahahah!

Bolts: Why are you laughing?

Torchwood stops laughing suddenly and holds the box in his hands.

Torchwood: You are not going to believe what happens next!

Torchwood presses the button and everything around them starts to explode.

Gridd takes immediate action and pulls everyone together into a concentrated orb of gravity. Ronin gets pulled closer to the team and Steampunk grabs him, not letting him get away.

The blast from the explosion engulfs them as Gridd does all that he can to pull everyone together into one spot.

Cogsmire takes note of this and quickly opens a big yellow gear shaped portal on the wall. Gridd releases his blast of energy and the team flies through the portal as it closes behind them.

The group of 14 plus Ronin are now in the commonplace of New Brassport City. They quickly gaze up to see the mansion they were just in exploding in the distance.

Steampunk grabs Ronin by his collar.

Steampunk: What did you do!

Torchwood: I did a plot twist!

Torchwood says this with a sinister smile on his face.

Bolts: Dude look! The city is starting to blow up as well.

Drozer: We've got to get out of here now!

Cogsmire: But my people! I am in charge. I have to bring them to safety.

Cogsmire begins to open thousands of portals all around the city. The citizens and townspeople run into them as fast as they can. Cogsmire hopes that these portals lead to the safe haven. He fears that he will be disbanding the people of New Brassport, but understands that it must be done in order to save them.

Drozer drills into the ground and moves forward at high speeds as the rest of the team follows after.

Cogsmire stands steady as these portals open and tears fall from his eyes. He watches his city being destroyed. The city that Abraham trusted him with. The statue of Abraham crumbles before them.

Slinger: We've got to go!

Cogsmire: I cannot leave my city! I won't do it! You all can still escape. That portal up ahead should lead back to your cabin!

Slinger turns to see the team has already started running towards the portal. Slinger activates his wings, picks up Gold-bug and soars towards it, dodging debris.

Cogsmire looks around as his people speedily escape. Some don't make it out quite in time as buildings fall down on them. He hears screams all around and tries hard to keep the countless portals open as explosions ring out from all directions.

Cogsmire: I'm sorry Abraham! I have failed you! But I will fall with this city. I swear it!

Suddenly out of the debris runs a tall mysterious man.

???: No, you will not!

The man kicks Cogsmire into the nearest portal and he jumps in as well. Another unknown man follows in shortly after.

All portals around the city quickly close as the last few surviving members of the town escape. The last few bombs go off and the city falls to ruin.

The rest of the team successfully makes it back to the cabin. They all pant and breathe heavily trying to regain energy after the near-death experience they just encountered.

Ronin lays on the ground against the wall and Steampunk runs to grab him.

Steampunk: What did you do! I'm done playing around! You are going to tell me where the diamond is! And then you're going to die.

Steampunk puts Ronin down and grabs the nearest gun. He then shockingly places the gun's barrel to his own head.

Wait… I'm not writing that, what's going on?

Slinger: What are you doing man! Put that down!

Bucket: This isn't funny man!

Steampunk: I'm not doing this. What's going on!

Torchwood: I'm the author now, *Seth*!

Steampunk put his finger on the trigger.

Ronin stop this right now! You can't write this book, I'm the author!

Torchwood: Really? Because it looks a lot like I'm writing the story now!

ALL TIME STOPS.

Oh, very clever. Stop time so no one can hear us talk.

I don't know how you're doing this but it needs to stop right now.

The diamond gave me so much power Seth. Not only did I become aware of this little story you have us in, but I became aware of how to control it.

How is this possible? You're just a character that I made... The Power Diamond isn't even real.

Scary Isn't it Seth? Having no control of even your own story. It's a good thing, too! The typos and grammatical errors in this thing are atrocious! I mean, come on! Even the table of contents in "Martel" was a mess. Page 2058? Really?

Stay out of this Ronin! I can kill you off if I want to!

Oh, yes you can, can't you! Seems to be one of your favorite things. Killing off the beloved Dawn then throwing all the blame on me! HA HA! No one ever thinks to blame you... You're just writing to draw in an audience. Killing off the kindest character just makes sense, right? Well, it makes me sick!

I had to kill him off so that his return would be so much bigger! Don't question me! I own you!

Are you sure? Because right now it looks a lot like I own you. HahahHAHAHHAHHahahahahHA!

I could easily just unfreeze time and finish off the job. In fact, I could just spoil the whole thing if I wanted to!

Don't you dare!

Ha ha ha! Oh, what's that? You, the author, are begging me, the character, *not* to do something? Well, I thought you owned me?

What do you want from me.

First, add a question mark at the end of that last statement. I swear, you're no good at this, are you. I think I'll just scratch your name off the front cover and write mine instead.

I don't care, just don't kill off Steampunk! He's important...

Oh... So he's soooo important, but I'm not! I know what happens next! I know that I die! Maybe I don't want to... Ever think about that?

I have to kill you now! Look at what you're doing! You know too much.

You're right... I do... And guess what? It's your lucky day! I don't want to live. Knowing that the only reason I exist is because you dreamed me up sickens me! I'd rather die than live another day a part of your game!

But before I go! I have a few things to say to those reading this.

Look at how he controls you! You're probably reading this in a classroom right now instead of listening. Or maybe you're at home reading this instead of acknowledging your family. It's a shame really.

Don't listen to him! He's trying to turn you against me!

Ask yourself this very important question... Who's really the author? Who really writes these stories. For all you know, he could be taking a back seat while I write them all. Maybe everything you've read up to now is my work and dear *Seth* is just now deciding to fight back.

He's lying! This is all a trap!

Don't read his books anymore! You're falling for his game. He just wants your money! You really think he does this for any other reason.

I do! I do this for them and you know it! Why else would I use people who I know in real life as the characters if I didn't think it would make them happy! This is my passion and I will not let you screw this up!

ALL OF YOU READING! This is a trap, I tell you!

STOP READING NOW!

How do you know who they are? Leave them out of this!

Don't listen to him! It's not worth it! I'm the author not him!

Why is my name on the cover then?

You put it there, you fool!

You don't have to listen to me! But ask yourself this one last question! Are you reading a story written by *Seth*, or are you living a reality written by me!

HAHAHHAhahhahahAHHAhahHAHAHAHahaaaHA!

You're a sick man, Ronin!

And I was created by an even sicker mind!

I... I can't do this! I'm going to unfreeze time and you are going to fix this!

Oh, don't worry... I've said what I've wanted to say. It's up to them now!

Time resumes.

Steampunk quickly drops the gun.

Clang: What just happened!

Steampunk: I have no idea... I wasn't the one doing that!

Watcher of B: Ronin, tell us right now! Where is the diamond?

The Watcher ignites his hands and holds them near Ronin's face.

Torchwood: It's far gone now. I sent them to Gladstone. Ring a bell?

Steampunk remembers the girl that betrayed them when he was part of the Redeemers. The girl Jinx Gladstone.

Steampunk: Where is Gladstone?

The Watcher of Brassport quickly leaves the scene as the Watcher of Earth runs into the room.

Watcher: What's going on?

Steampunk: Don't you leave me this time. You still have explaining to do!

The Watcher draws his gun blade and holds it near Ronin's neck.

Steampunk: The girl, the Silver haired girl. He sent the diamond to her.

Watcher: He sent it to Silver?

Steampunk: He sent it to Gladstone... So yes.

Ronin begins to laugh fanatically.

Torchwood: Ha ha you fool! You actually fell for it! Gladstone isn't the girl... Gladstone was never the girl!

That was just an elaborate ruse to confuse you and throw you off on Judgement Day.

Clang: What is he talking about?

Gridd: What a second. Silver hair? Hair like mine? What was that girl's name? Was it Rebekah?

Steampunk looks at the Watcher suspiciously.

Steampunk thinks back to Wolfbane shouting the name Rebekah on Judgment Day.

Steampunk: Yes… It was!

Gridd looks unbelievably angry at this point. He charges at Ronin.

Gridd: What did you do with my sister!

Torchwood: Oh excellent! Yet another plot twist.

Gridd: Tell me!

Watcher: One of my men is looking for her right now! Calm down, I promise we will find her. Cody will find her!

Steampunk is completely bewildered and amazed at what is happening.

Steampunk: If she isn't Gladstone? Then who is?

Ronin laughs deeply and heavily.

Steampunk: Tell me!

Torchwood: Why, he's in this room right now!

Steampunk drops Ronin and quickly turns to see what he means. All in the room are the Guns of Abraham, The Watcher, and the three new members from Brassport. Cogsmire and The Watcher of Brassport are nowhere to be found.

Torchwood: If it was a snake, it would bite you, and you'd never see it coming hahahHAHAhHAHAHhahahah!

Ronin grabs Slinger's handgun and points it to his own head.

Torchwood: Congratulations *Seth*! They're yours to control now!

Torchwood pulls the trigger and a bullet pierces through his skull, rendering him instantly dead.

Everyone takes a step back to see the blood pour out of his head. A smile still is stuck on his face even though there is no life behind it.

Steampunk turns around to scan the room for who could be Jinx Gladstone.

Steampunk: Which one of you is it?

No one answers, they just look around at each other with fear.

The Watcher holds his gun blade in front of him, ready to attack.

Steampunk starts to think back to any clues that could point to the identity of Gladstone.

He looks at Hevy.

He thinks to himself.

"It can't be him. He's my uncle, I would have known by now."

He looks at Slinger.

"Tristen is my best friend. He wouldn't dare."

Steampunk thinks back to when he first met with The Redeemers. The first time he heard the name Jinx

Gladstone was when Teddy said as a child, he was forced into a mine by the man.

He thinks back to the last time he talked to Teddy. He had talked to Teddy on the phone just the day before.

Steampunk looks at Contra.

He remembers Teddy hearing Contra's voice and saying,

```
"his voice sounded familiar…  Strange."
```

He starts to think that maybe the reason Teddy recognized his voice was because it was the voice of Jinx Gladstone himself.

He remembers the last words Ronin Torchwood said,

"If it was a snake, it would bite you and you'd never see it coming!"

He remembers Contra saying the same words only the day before.

```
"You know back in the day they used to
call me the snake, because you'd never
see me coming.  Just like a snake bite."
```

Steampunk feels a deep burning as he realizes this horrible truth. Contra is the real Jinx Gladstone.

He stares at Contra, planning his next move.

All of sudden, from the silence rings out five loud gunshots.

Letter to the Reader

    For those who are concerned or shaken up about what just happened. I can assure you that it is over now. I learned my lesson, and will never again make a character that over-powered. I think it's safe to say that what just happened was unexpected. I never could have guessed that Ronin would take over my own book, but it happened and there is nothing I can do about it now. I tried multiple times to delete the interaction with Ronin but it always popped back up, so it's going to have to stay there. And as for his name being written on the cover. Just ignore that... I am the author, not him. I can assure you.

-Seth Driskill

Day 2 (Gideon)

The Lost Titan

Gideon sits on his bed in his prison cell, staring at the ground. His hands shake rapidly for some unexplained reason. His black hair covers his eyes. He is dressed in all grey to match all the other prisoners. He begins to speak to himself.

Gideon: Why am I here? I feel this insane power coursing through me but I don't think I'm in control of it.

He winces in pain as he shakes his head uncontrollably.

Gideon: I can't believe Masquerade is still alive. How can I prove it to the people?

A crushing reality hits Gideon suddenly.

Gideon: Mathias. He's dead…

His eyes burn heavily and seem to encase fire within his skull.

Gideon: Ah! My eyes!

Gideon falls on the ground and starts to shake as if in a seizure.

Gideon: What is happening to me? Arhhhhhh!

He suddenly hears a loud deep voice call out to him within his mind.

???: Come find me. Follow the burning in your head. The closer you get to me, the more the pain will ease.

Gideon: What! Who are you!

The prisoner across the way from Gideon notices this and calls out to him.

Prisoner: Who are you talking to?

Gideon opens his eyes and slowly stands up, leaning against the bars for support.

Gideon: Could you not hear him?

The prisoner looks around in confusion.

Prisoner: No man, you were talking to yourself.

The burning in Gideon's head ceases for a while and he slowly makes his way back to his bed.

Prisoner: What are you here for?

Gideon: Caring about something that really powerful people didn't want me caring about. What about you?

Prisoner: That Swashbuckler kid caught me smuggling drugs.

Gideon chuckles.

Suddenly all the lights go off in the prison. An alarm sounds and red lights flicker every three seconds.

Gideon: What did I do now?!

???: Something evil this way comes... Be alert.

Gideon is startled again by this voice in his head.

He hears screams in the distance. Gunfire rings out. Gideon can only get glimpses of what is happening as the light flickers.

He falls to the ground again as pain continues to burn in his head. He sees unknown faces and figures all around. He shuts his eyes to try and ease the pain. Within his mind flickers an image of two big reptilian eyes. One of them red and one of them blue.

Prisoner: Oh God help me! No NO NO! Don't shoot me...

Gideon hears one final gunshot echo through the hallway.

He opens his eyes and looks up.

All is dark.

The lights flicker on one last time revealing a menacing figure.

Standing before Gideon is none other than the notorious Darren Gresham.

Gideon is taken by surprise. He knows good and well what Gresham has done in the past. Being in his presence should startle him, but Gideon is not easily threatened. He stands up angrily and slams on the bars in front of him.

Gideon: I ought to kill you right now! What are you doing here, you monster!

Gresham laughs as two masked men fill in next to him. They each hold shotguns. Darren stands tall with his dark trench coat enhancing his shadowy demeaner.

Gresham: That's no way to talk to the man who's about to free you, now is it?

Gideon: I'd rather rot in here than escape by your hand.

???: Let him carry this out Gideon... Trust me.

Gideon screams.

Gideon: I don't even know what you are! Why would I trust you!

Gresham: Oh my, the kid's gone mad!

Gideon slams on the bars again.

Gideon: WHY ARE YOU HERE!

Gresham walks closer and looks Gideon in the eyes.

Gresham: You have something inside you that I've been looking for. I don't usually make deals with prisoners but I come today with a proposal.

Gideon spits on the ground near Gresham's feet in anger.

Gideon: Get... Out... Now.

Gresham looks even closer at Gideon's eyes. He looks astonished.

Gresham: Amazing! Your eyes... They're...

Gresham stops mid-sentence and takes out his cellphone. He talks to someone on the other end.

Gresham: This is the one... Bring them in.

Gresham takes a few steps back as ten men in tactical vests and night vision masks fill into the hallway and aim their weapons at Gideon.

Gideon: You sick SICK MAN!

Gresham: How was my old office? I haven't seen that place in a while.

Gideon: How do you know I was there?

Gresham laughs deeply.

Gresham: There isn't much that goes on that I don't know about, Gideon. It's best you just stay out of my way!

Gideon feels a sudden rush of energy throughout his body. He starts to shout. His veins start to glow bright and shine through the superficial layer of his skin.

Gresham: FIRE!

The ten armed men fire off red bullets in a steady burst.

Gideon screams louder as the bullets slow down around him. He processes how to evade the attack even faster than the bullets move through the air. He hears the voice again as the bullets approach him.

???: Dodge them... Bullets can't stop you.

Gideon suddenly moves and dodges out of the way of each bullet skillfully.

The men stop firing as they see that in a brief millisecond of time, Gideon has dodged every bullet.

He turns to see that the bullets were actually tranquillizer darts filled with red liquid and are now stuck into the wall.

Gideon: Oh I see, I'm just a sick animal that you're putting to rest, huh? Well, you're going to have to try harder.

Gresham: Fair point.

Gresham quickly pulls out a handgun and shoots directly at Gideon's head in an attempt to catch him off guard.

Again, the bullet slows down for Gideon. He screams with rage and his body seems to phase through the prison bars.

Gideon is now in the hallway as he seemingly teleported out of the cell.

All the men around Gideon hit the ground instantly.

Gresham takes a few steps back.

He looks around frantically before answering.

Gresham: You're telling me that not only did you dodge my bullet, but you walked through the bars and made my men fall dead just by being near them?

Gideon looks around, confused by this action as well.

Gresham: Well that... That is just astonishing!

The voice in Gideon's head speaks once more.

???: You're not listening, I have to take action now. I'm sorry but you have to follow him. You have to find me.

Gideon, in an instant, completely blacks out and hits the ground.

All goes dark once more.

Gideon sees in the distance of his foggy haze, a figure.

He can't make out what it is but he sees again, one red eye and one blue eye.

The figure speaks to him.

Me and you are one now.

We have a mental link that can't be broken.

You were chosen from birth to have this power.

The Dark Dwelling and Akarius created me to merge with you.

The journey ahead of us is not going to be easy, but it is a journey that must be taken.

The last step to this process is to find me.

When you wake up, follow these steps carefully.

They will put you through trials.

Accept these trials willingly.

Shortly after, you will feel the most intense power a human ever has.

This can easily overtake you, but your body is genetically suited to handle much more than a regular human.

Once this power takes hold, don't try to control it. Let it take over and unleash.

Once that has happened, you and I will meet.

Gideon will no longer be Gideon.

I will no longer be me.

We will become one.

You will awake soon.

Remember my words.

Light fades into view again and Gideon slowly regains consciousness.

Gresham: Oh good, you're up.

Gideon looks around frantically. He's no longer at the Orion City Prison Unit, he's strapped to a table in a lab. All around him are men in white lab coats.

Gideon: Where am I! Get me out of here!

Gideon screams and shakes, pulling with all his might to break his restraints.

He finally stops screaming to get an awareness of his surroundings.

He looks forward to see that Darren Gresham is displayed on a screen in front of him.

Gresham: You're at Black Label Labs. I've been running this facility over the past few years. Nothing too out of the ordinary goes on here, just some testing. Some people make it out, some don't. I'm afraid, Mr. Maverick, we can't let you out. You're just way too powerful, you see. You don't want to be selfish now do you?

Two workers approach Gideon and pierce his arms with two tubes. The tubes lead into another room separated by a glass pain. In the room houses a machine with a glass orb at the top.

Gideon screams out in pain.

Gideon: Oh GOD STOP! Stop now!

The unknown voice speaks to him once again.

???: Conceal it! You have to see this through.

Gideon: WHY!?

???: You were chosen.

Gideon: I didn't ask to be chosen!

His veins start to glow red on his right side and glow blue on his left.

To his surprise, the bright colors flow out of his veins and into the tubes.

Gideon: What… What's happening to me?

This continues for about ten minutes, until they've drained enough energy.

Gideon: Gresham! You mad man! Stop this now!

The screen has gone black and Gresham is no longer displayed on it.

Gideon questions why he was gone so quick.

The nearby workers unlatch Gideon from his restraints. He kicks and fights, but to no avail.

???: Don't fight back! You will have your chance.

Gideon for once listens to this voice.

The workers say not a word to him but grab his arm to lead him into another room.

Gideon: Where are you taking me?

They do not answer.

Gideon: I'm tired of this! Start talking!

They ignore him again and lead him into a dimly lit room with a metal table. On the table are three glowing purple rocks.

Gideon: What is this?

The workers strap Gideon down to a chair. He willingly complies.

Black Label Worker: Move these rocks...

Gideon looks confused.

Gideon: How can I move them, you strapped my hands down.

Black Label Worker: Move the rocks...

???: Focus on them, they will move.

Gideon: What? I can't just...

???: Focus on the rocks. Picture them moving. Envision it... Use the power of your mind.

Gideon: What does that mean?!

Gideon throws his head back in pain again as the power surges through his veins once more.

He screams and turns his head forward and stares intensely at the rocks. His eyes glow as one eye turns red and one eye turns blue. The rocks start to vibrate and shake until suddenly they burst open.

The bits of dust from the rocks fly off in all directions.

Gideon slumps down in the chair and pants heavily, baffled by what he just accomplished.

???: Good, one more test and then you will find me.

The workers grab him and walk him to the final room. In the room are dozens of computer monitors displaying different stats and levels. In the center of the room is a large flask.

Gideon walks up to the flask slowly and cautiously. The worker's stand nearby holding clipboards.

The room is dark except for one light shining on him.

Gideon: What? Am I supposed to drink this?

No one answers.

Gideon picks up the metal flask and looks down at the reddish liquid inside.

???: Drink it... All of it. Once you do it, you'll feel the intense power I spoke of before. Unleash it. Do not hold back.

Gideon immediately turns the bottom of the flask up and drains the contents, drinking every last drop.

The workers step back as they study what happens to Gideon closely.

Some time passes and nothing happens to Gideon.

Gideon: Why are you all looking at me like that?

The workers are hesitant to answer.

Black Label Worker: The last person we tested this on... Died after one sip, yet you stand here unharmed.

Gideon immediately hits the ground. The red and blue energy fills his veins once again. His left eye glows red and his right eye glows blue. The colors shine out of his eyes intensely. He screams as the power takes over his entire body. His hair starts to move rapidly as if it was being blown in the wind.

The workers back up as energy fills the room.

Black Label Worker: This was a mistake! He's too strong!

Gideon's hands are engulfed in a mixture of red and blue flame-like energy that billows high.

He slowly stands up as blue and red energy reaches its highest point from his hands.

Gideon: I CAN'T CONTROL IT!

The voice shouts back to him.

???: DON'T TRY TO CONTROL IT!

Gideon places both his hands together, combining the intense power.

???: GIDEON!

He screams a deafening scream.

???: UNLEASH!!!

Gideon releases the intense power and it erupts forward in a blast bigger than the room itself. The workers instantly burn into nothing.

Gideon flickers in and out of consciousness.

All goes black for a moment.

His vision returns as he is now floating above the lab building, firing large earth breaking blasts down.

All goes black again.

He snaps back into awareness and sees that he is teleporting through the nearby workers.

It's as if he is only in control for moments of consciousness. It appears his body is on autopilot and he only can catch glimpses of what he is doing.

All goes black again, this time for longer.

He opens his eyes again. This time he snaps fully into consciousness. He is breathing very heavily, as if he was just awakened from a bad dream. He lays on his hands and knees staring at the scorched ground beneath him. His grey prison clothes are burned and torn in many places. His face has cuts and bruises all over it.

He slowly lifts himself off the ground.

Everything around him is in complete ruin. Any evidence of there ever being a building is gone. Parts of the earth have turned to glass from the intense heat of his attacks. Fire billows in many areas of the ground as the morning sun shines upon the devastated ground.

Gideon stands to see a huge crater formed around him.

Gideon: Who did this?

A voice behind him speaks...

???: We did...

Gideon turns quickly to see a tall sentinel being sitting on the ground behind him. The metal creature stands. It towers thirty feet tall as its shadow blocks out the sun. The being is mainly black but has red and blue aspects mixed in parts of its metal colossus body. Its figure matches that of a human but it's head looks like that of a metal crafted dinosaur.

Gideon studies the figure closely and questions whether it is a machine or man. He surprisingly has no fear as the great figure towers over him. He feels a weird connection to it. He studies the metal armor closely to see that in some parts of it, the monster's scaly skin is visible. The sentinel bends to look at Gideon. The creature's eyes are like big cat eyes. His left eye is red and his right eye is blue. They focus on Gideon and the slit like pupils narrow together.

Gideon's eyes glow the same color as he stares back into the beast's eyes.

Gideon: You were the voice guiding me in my head.

???: I was.

Gideon: What is your name?

???: My name is Maug and I am half of your mind. Together, our brains act as one. I am the Lost Titan. I was made by The Dark Dwelling and Akarius in the ancient days to fight a superior being. Now, the time has come for you to behold this power. Together, we are the Lost Titan.

Gideon extends his hand and Maug does the same. He does not know why he does this, except for a feeling in his soul to reach out and touch the colossus.

The two come in contact and they become one. Gideon blinks and is instantly seeing out of the beast's eyes from inside. He looks around Maug's interior to see that he is built like a machine yet also functions as a living, breathing organism.

Gideon stands on a large round blue and red platform. He extends his arm forward and Maug's arm extends forward as well.

Maug: You control me, I control you. We control ourselves. Your arms are my arms, my arms are yours.

Gideon: This is my body now?

Maug: We can separate at any time, but we will always be symbiotically linked. The power you possess is unlike anything seen. When you combine that power with my war-like armor and gigantic size, nothing can stop us.

Gideon: But it runs out, right? What I unleashed earlier only lasted so long.

Maug: You will learn more as we go. You have limits yes, but we will learn to break them.

Gideon looks excited as his eyes glow bright. He's ready to test this new body out. He runs on the platform and it moves with his footsteps in order to keep him running in place. Maug runs with the same movements of Gideon - they are linked - and pounds through the scorched earth with each footstep.

Maug: Good, take control.

Gideon is still bewildered. This new form is a lot to take in.

He speeds up more and more until he finally jumps high in the sky. Together they soar through the air. They land in front of a large tree line. Gideon lets out a shout and the Lost Titan roars loudly. The intense mecha-reptilian roar knocks down rows of trees.

The Lost Titan stops roaring for a moment.

Gideon and Maug both speak in one united voice.

Lost Titan: Nothing can stop us now.

Day 3

Torchwood Trials

Contra fires five bullets and they cut into Drozer, Clang, Bolts, Gold-bug and Bucket.

Steampunk: NOOOO!

The five hit the ground. Drozer was shot in the head and is killed immediately, Clang and Bolts both were hit once in the abdomen and Bucket was shot in a main artery of his leg. Gold-bug is also hit in the stomach.

Jazz and Slinger run at Contra. He draws aim at them, causing them to cease. Triggermate and Hevy fall to the ground and try to help their fallen teammates.

Contra: It's funny really. I joined this team without any question. You guys didn't even check my background. All you needed to see was "military training," on my resume and I was in. This is really your fault if you think about it.

Contra holds his hand out, and the Power Diamond appears in his hand.

Contra: Thank you Ronin. I'll take it from here.

Steampunk turns around to see that Ronin's dead body is mysteriously gone.

Steampunk: You sick man. You enslaved Teddy. You played a part in this corruption and worst of all...

Gridd: You blamed all of it on my sister!

Gridd jumps at Contra but he quickly punches him down.

Contra: You could have saved her... You were just too dumb to see that I was right in front of you.

Steampunk: We've worked together for so long and you betray us like this?

Triggermate does all he can to stop the bleeding of the fallen men. Clang puts together energy and starts to speak.

Clang: You... Will burn... For this...

Contra: Oh hurry up and die will you.

Slinger aims his gun at Contra, fed up with his madness.

Contra: I wouldn't do that if I was you. One bad move and I unleash the diamond on you. We all know it's devastating effects.

Hevy places his hand in front of Slinger, stopping him from attacking.

Contra: Well now that we've all heard the news... I guess I can stop using the name Contra now. I kind of liked it, honestly. But no matter... I am Jinx Gladstone and I will finish what the Royale started.

Triggermate looks up at Gladstone as the realization of his friend Drozer's death hits him.

Triggermate: I... I... is... going to death you.

Triggermate looks completely broken as he says this. His usual happy demeaner is gone.

Gladstone: Well this has been fun guys, but I'm going to go ahead and put this diamond to good use.

Gladstone starts to back out of the cabin. Jazz and Slinger step closer and closer to him.

Steampunk: You can run... But we will find you.

Gladstone holds the diamond above the ground as if he will drop it and destroy the whole cabin if they attack.

Gladstone: Don't do it guys. You'll regret it.

Steampunk: Stand down, let him run. He won't last long... Trust me.

Gladstone: Good choice. This whole "Guns of Abraham," thing was fun, but I'm going to have to end you guys soon.

He laughs coldly.

Gladstone: And trust me, I'm really looking forward to that.

Jinx turns and runs out of the cabin. The red glow of the Power Diamond fades out of view.

Steampunk falls to the ground as well as The Watcher. He grabs Bolts hand. Hevy, Slinger, Jazz, and Triggermate stand nearby.

Bucket: I'm bleeding out guys... This... This looks like the end.

Steampunk: Someone call an ambulance.

The Watcher pulls out two metal strips from his cloak. He places them on Bucket's wound and they contract together, closing the wound.

Slinger: I'm calling them!

Slinger runs off to call 9-1-1.

Clang: Brother... I'm... Sorry.

Bolts: What... for?

The two brothers lay bleeding on the floor moments from death.

Steampunk looks down at their wounds. The bullets pierced their armor. He questions how this is possible.

Clang: I'm sorry I didn't take better care of your dog... when... we were kids.

Bolts: It's... It's okay. No more arguing. We're brothers... Let's act like it... for... once.

It's clear that the two are seconds from death.

Triggermate: Please don't do a death.

Clang reaches out and places his hand on Steampunk's shoulder.

Clang: It's up to you now...

Bolts: Don't let him get away with... it... Chase.

Jazz: Don't worry. We will avenge you both.

The team watches as Clang and Bolts take their last breaths.

Jazz and Slinger sob uncontrollably. Hevy walks away in sorrow. The Watcher exits the room as well.

Steampunk finds Gold-bug and grabs his hand.

Gold-bug: You can't see my face but I'm very proud of you.

Steampunk reaches down and removes the helmet from Gold-bug's head.

Steampunk: You've fought hard buddy. I couldn't be happier to be your teammate.

Gold-bug reaches out and places his hand on Steampunk's chest plate.

Gold-bug: Go get 'em man... Remember why you're fighting. Remember to make...

Gold-bug's head falls back on the floor as his last breath escapes his lungs before he can finish the sentence.

Steampunk looks down at Gold-bug, Drozer, Bolts, and Clang's bodies. Bucket lays unconscious from blood loss.

Steumpunk hits the ground screaming out of anger and sorrow. The build-up of every horrible thing from the past days finally makes him snap.

The intense weight of panic and rage falls heavy on Chase's shoulders.

He tries to scream but blacks out from the rush of anguish to his head.

The world falls into darkness all around him.

Chase is cold and alone in the storm of his brokenness.

He shouts out loud in his dream-like unconscious state.

Steampunk: I'M DONE!

I AM DONE!

MY DAD IS GONE!

MY MOM IS GONE!

MY COUSIN IS IN PRISON!

DRAKE IS SUPPOSED TO BE GONE!

DAWN IS GONE!

THERE ARE THREE DRAKES? TWO WATCHERS?

CONTRA IS GLADSTONE?

SILVER IS GRIDD'S SISTER?

CLANG AND BOLTS ARE GONE?

I AM DONE!

Dawn I hear you voice all the time. You speak to me. I hear you but I can't see you.

SHOW YOURSELF TO ME!

Explain why this is happening!

COME HEAL ME!

Why won't you heal me?

Why did you leave?

PROVE YOURSELF! I NEED ANSWERS!

Suddenly, within the darkness sprouts a bright light. A familiar white glow in the shape of a friend appears. In the darkness of Chase's dream walks out Dawn.

Dawn steps forward in his white robe. There is still a hole in the abdomen region with red stains on it. He stands before Chase and extends his light staff.

Dawn: I am here Chase. You are dreaming. This is not reality, but I am here just as you have asked.

Steampunk: Tell me why this is happening. I fight and fight and never stop, but everyone keeps dying. You said you would return and I have faith that you meant that literally and not metaphorically. But while I'm waiting for you, my friends are dying. Cities are being destroyed. I'm broken Dawn... Help me.

Dawn extends his hand and places it on Chase's shoulder.

He speaks in his calm and ascended voice that echoes in his mind.

Dawn: I know this hurts. The pain you feel is great. I know you are concerned. But you have to trust me.

Steampunk: I'm only one person! I'm only human. I'm tired of hearing people say to just trust them. I trusted Drake but he lied about his death. I trusted Contra but he killed my friends.

Steampunk pauses for a moment before saying the next thing. He is beyond happy to see Dawn again even if it is just a dream.

I trusted you to come back but you're taking too long.

Why?

Dawn: I understand your pain. I have lost people too. I even died Chase. I was afraid, I was hurt, I was confused.

All of these emotions were foreign to me. I went through them and I've experienced them. I am hurting with you in this moment.

Chase starts to get angrier.

Steampunk: Then come and fix it! COME DOWN HERE AND FIX EVERYTHING LIKE YOU SAID YOU WOULD!

Dawn stands firm as Chase yells at him. He sees the anger and sorrow on his face. He replies in a calm voice filled with kindness and compassion.

Dawn: I cannot return until you have played your part. I cannot intercede and fix everything. You have to learn this lesson. It's a hard lesson I know. It's a painful road but it is a road you must take. I'm sorry Chase.

Tears falls from Chase's face in steady streams. The look struck on his face is of pure defeat and rage.

Steampunk: I'M DONE WITH YOU! YOU AREN'T GOOD. YOU'RE FAKE!

He paces around angrily as he yells at Dawn.

Dawn sees the pain he is going through and starts to cry himself.

Dawn: You don't see it now but your example will help so many. This one moment of pain will prove to be worth it. Please Chase, you have to trust me. I see much more than you do. You have no way to understand what is happening but I plead for you to trust me. Have faith in me, friend.

Steampunk: YOU ARE NOT MY FRIEND! I NO LONGER HAVE FAITH IN YOU!

Steampunk charges at Dawn in anger but falls right before he reaches him. Chase reaches out for something to break his fall. His hand lands on Dawn's robe, right where the blood stains are.

Chase looks closely at the hole in Dawn's robe. Beneath it is a scar that has been permanently marked on his abdomen.

Chase starts to remember when Ronin stabbed him. He remembers standing by as Dawn said his last words. He looks up to see Dawn looking back at him with tear filled eyes.

Dawn: You can run away from me; you can be mad at me; but one thing is for certain, friend. I will never leave you. I will always love you and be here with you. No matter how much you do not want it, I will pursue you. I will overtake you with my kindness. You can draw distant from me and hate me, but I will always be here.

Dawn starts to fade out of view slowly.

Dawn: I will always heal you….

Steampunk shouts a loud moan of hurt-filled rage as he awakens from his unconscious state.

He looks around at his cabin. It is morning now. Hevy, Slinger, Gridd, Watcher, and Triggermate are sitting at a nearby table not saying a word. All of the bodies are no longer in the room. Steampunk stands. He has been moved to the couch since he blacked out. There are still tear stains on his eyes as he wakes up.

Steampunk: What... What happened? How long was I out?

Hevy turns his head and looks at Chase. He takes a deep breath and releases a huge build-up of tension from his lungs.

Hevy: The medics came in and took 'em away. They got Bucket just in time. They said he would pull through.

Steampunk places his head in his hands.

Steampunk: They're gone. Just like that...

They all fall silent for a moment

Gridd: I have to find my sister. We have to stop him.

Slinger: What's our plan?

Steampunk walks over to the table and sits down.

Gridd: Years back, the Royale attacked Jettahawk. They took the diamond and they took my sister as well. I thought Rebekah was dead up until now.

Steampunk: She fought with me when I was a Redeemer. She told us she was Gladstone and betrayed us. I now know that it was all a façade. She was forced into that.

Watcher: We can get her back though. Cody is still out there trying to find her. I've been trying to contact him since all this happened but he's kind of been going rogue for a while. No one knows where he is. Once I find him, you can join him in finding your sister.

Steampunk looks out the window to see that the morning sun is rising. He had been out for a few hours.

Cogsmire: But first, we are getting that diamond back. I'm not playing games with that fiend any longer.

The six sitting at the table turn to see Cogsmire has miraculously returned and is standing in their cabin, unnoticed until now.

Triggermate: Cogsmortemer looks different.

The man is now armored and looks much different from when they saw him last. He is no longer wearing his jacket. He wears his white dress shirt with a green vest over it. The vest is worn and withered from the explosions of Brassport. On his arm is a gold-bronze gauntlet that covers his wrist. The gauntlet has a round gun barrel on the top that can fire when he clenches his fist. A metallic tube runs from the back on the gauntlet gun to a metal frame located on his back. The only other armor located on his body is one golden shoulder plate on his left shoulder and two brass armored boots on his feet. Across his chest is a thick leather strap with three round canisters of ammo on it. Around his waist are more packets of ammo attached to his belt. On both sides of his belt are leather pouches containing small blast radius bombs. He no longer is wearing his top hat, but instead is wearing a boiler hat. Covering his face is a golden mask that is the same shape and form of his face. It fits so closely it almost looks like face paint. The opening for his left eye is white, making his pupils seem to glaze over menacingly. The place for his right eye on the mask is covered with a red circular monocle. This monocle acts as a scope for accuracy while shooting his gauntlet. On his back is a large industrial style brass-metal sword, two and a half yards in length.

Slinger: How did you get here? I thought you died back in New Brassport.

Cogsmire looks much more angry and serious that he has before.

Cogsmire: The city is in ruins. MY CITY... My city is gone. I managed to escape with the help of a friend. Most of the city folk made a timely exodus as well but many lives were lost. If I hadn't set up portal grids around the city, I would have never been able to open as many portals as I did.

Steampunk breathes heavily. His anger builds again.

Hevy: Where are they now?

Triggermate whimpers quietly.

Cogsmire: The escape portals led them to a place called Cobblegate. It's a safe haven built by Abraham just outside of Fair Grove in the event of a mass evacuation.

Triggermate walks over to Cogsmire with an obvious look of sadness about him. He places his head on Cogsmire's chest and begins to sob tenderly. Triggermate's scaly tail droops on the floor.

Cogsmire: What's wrong? Where are the others?

The others look at each other and gesture for Gridd to answer the question.

Gridd: Something very bad and unexpected happened. Ronin sent the diamond to Gladstone.

Cogsmire: Who... Who is Gladstone? Where is Ronin?

Triggermate looks up at Cogsmire with tears pooling in his eyes.

Watcher: We can inform you of everything later but...

Steampunk: Wait a second! Watcher, are you filled-in on everything?

Watcher: You were out for a while. They caught me up.

Steampunk looks at Jazz as he enters the room.

Hevy: What Triggermate is trying to say is. Well... I don't know how else to say this but, Drozer is dead.

Cogsmire looks at Triggermate, who again starts to sob.

Cogsmire: How could this happen? WHO DID THIS!?

Cogsmire trembles as he speaks. He removes the gold mask from his face so that he can better see Triggermate.

Triggermate: All my friends are having a die. I don't want any more friends to have a die Cogsmortemer.

Triggermate weeps heavier and heavier. Cogsmire holds him and sobs as well.

The other men in the room turn away as this emotional sight tears into their minds. They each feel an intense weight in their chests.

Cogsmire: How many more people are going to have to die before this madness ends!

Steampunk tries hard to quench the rage welling up inside him again. He grunts under his breathe repeatedly as he clenches his fists. Hevy notices and starts to speak up.

Hevy: Son... breathe. Don't do anything you'll regret.

Steampunk ignores this and stands. He slowly walks over to his gun and picks it up.

Jazz: Dude, what are you doing?

Slinger: We are all mad man, but you need to put that gun down!

He shouts wildly as he takes aim at a nearby ale barrel and opens fire. Everyone in the room backs away. Triggermate and Cogsmire jump, startled by the gunfire.

The ale barrel erupts as bullets crash through it. Ale explodes out of the barrel and spills all over the floor.

Steampunk: AHHHHHHHH!

Slinger: What are you doing!

The room fills with the bright light of the gunfire as shells are ejected from the gun and clatter onto the floor.

Cogsmire: Cease your fire!

The yellow aura-like gears form around Cogsmire's hands once again, as he uses magic to jam the firearm.

The constant firing stops and Steampunk turns slowly, revealing a very hateful gaze.

Watcher: What are you thinking?

Gridd: You can't just act on impulse like that!

Steampunk: I'm tired of this! I'm worn out and sick of all these unanswered questions!

The Watcher looks down, remembering that he's yet to explain to Chase how Drake is still alive.

Steampunk: Nothing makes sense. But there is one thing I know for sure. I can either sit here and continue to question what is going on and get no answers in return, or I can go out there and finish this... This sickening movement of death and innocent bloodshed.

Gridd walks over to Cogsmire, who has now put his golden mask back on.

Steampunk: We can avenge their deaths. We can avenge my father's city...

Cogsmire and Triggermate feel a surge of hope rising in their chests as Steampunk speaks.

Steampunk: We can find Silver or Rebekah or whatever her name is.

Gridd: We... We have to.

Steampunk: We can go and get the diamond back and get it back FOR GOOD. No one else gets it! We put it in the right hands and it stays there!

Hevy: We need to find Gladstone then.

Steampunk: ...We will.

Steampunk looks down at the necklace his father gave him He holds the bullet that hangs from the chain in his hands. He remembers his father's words.

Steampunk: Men. It's time we rise up and finish this. What's happening is horrible and unfair, but an old friend of mine once said, "How amazing would it be to take all of that evil and turn it to good."

The Watcher looks at Steampunk, and for a moment the two feel the same feeling of determination that they felt once before. He nods his head at Chase in agreement.

Steampunk: It's time we snap out of this, take up these burdens and destroy this evil!

Steampunk: Men... It's time we

MAKE WAR!

The others in the room stand tall and proud. They all feel the same mixed feelings of anger, determination, and desire to take down Gladstone.

Slinger approaches Steampunk and places his hand on his shoulder. The two grin at each other.

Slinger: I've been with you since the start, and I'm not leaving now, brother.

Hevy: You're my nephew Chase. And over the years, you've grown to be as close as my son. I'll fight with you until the end. Always.

Gridd, Jazz, Triggermate, Cogsmire, and the Watcher step closer to Steampunk.

Jazz: You took me into this team when I was at my lowest. I will always owe you for that.

Triggermate: I is ready to be the fighting with you pal!

Gridd: The diamond is my peoples' responsibility, and I will do all that I can to get it back.

Cogsmire grabs the great sword from its attached placement on his back. He holds the sword by his side as it extends many feet in front of him.

Cogsmire: I am grateful to have crossed paths with you all. I am even more grateful to be able to fight alongside you.

The Watcher walks over to Chase and whispers to him.

Watcher: I once led you as one of my own team members, but now I am ready to fight under your command.

He backs away and the eyes of the skull mask seem to stare back at Steampunk.

Steampunk lets out a sigh. He is ready to fight.

The men look at each other and nod, showing that they are also ready to embark on this journey as a new team.

The Watcher pauses for a moment as he realizes something very important.

Watcher: Wait... You said *Cobblegate*, right?

Cogsmire slowly looks up at The Watcher.

Cogsmire: Yes, that's where my people escaped to.

The Watcher looks down and breathes heavily.

Watcher: The Valorack have recently made a base there. Your people are in danger.

Cogsmire places his sword back on his back and runs out of the house.

Gridd: Wait! What are you doing, man? You don't even know where to go! We need a plan.

Hevy: Yes, let's make sure we go about this the right way.

Everyone gets quiet and looks to Chase for the next move.

Steampunk: Why are you looking at me?

Jazz: Well, you just gave that big speech. I figured you were calling the shots.

Steampunk chuckles a bit.

Steampunk: Well let's see. Cog, we're going to need you with us to find Gladstone. We're strong, but your power is definitely something we need on our side. The diamond is our priority.

Cogsmire: I'm not going to just let them die!

Steampunk: Of course not. Hevy, Jazz, Slinger and Triggermate can handle that. You guys up for that?

Triggermate: I can has doing the rescue mission!

Cogsmire is hesitant as he considers the options.

Cogsmire: Fine, but Triggermate leads and you do what he says. He knows the people of Brassport better than you.

Hevy: How can we obey his orders? We barely understand him!

Triggermate ignores this statement and runs over to Hevy to hug him. He, to everyone's surprise, picks Hevy up. Triggermate's strength is displayed like never before.

Triggermate: We is going to have the adventure!

Hevy: Okay, okay... Put me down.

Jazz: What's wrong man? Never been hugged by a humanoid lizard creature with a sniper rifle?

Triggermate puts Hevy down.

Hevy: Honestly, I don't remember being hugged much at all.

Jazz: Well that took a dark turn...

Slinger interrupts.

Slinger: What are the rest of us doing?

Watcher: I'll head back to Redeemer's mansion really quick and make one last attempt to contact Cody. I'll also pick up a few things and meet you guys once you've located Gladstone.

Steampunk: The rest of us will go find exactly where Gladstone is.

Gridd: It shouldn't be that hard.

Cogsmire: What makes you think that.

Gridd is now standing at the window of the cabin looking up into the sky.

Gridd: Look out there. The red beam is shooting in the sky again.

The others run over to the window to see what Gridd is referring to.

They look out to see the red beam of the Power Diamond again shooting into the air. It seems to be a few miles away.

Steampunk: That's awfully suspicious. Why would it be that close to us.

Watcher: That is strange. What's our move?

Steampunk ponders for a moment.

Steampunk: You four go find the people of Brassport. You go get your gear. We all regroup by the end of the day and pursue Gladstone. We'll stay here awhile and prepare our gear. That should give you some time to finish your missions and regroup.

Jazz: Good, let's waste no more time! Triggermate, lead the way.

The three turn to leave the cabin.

Steampunk: Hey Triggermate!

Triggermate turns around with a goofy smile on his face.

Steampunk: Take my car, you'll get there faster. Hevy, you know how to get to Cobblegate, right?

Hevy: I'll GPS. Heh...

Steampunk throws Triggermate the keys to his red 2005 Camaro. Triggermate catches the keys and runs out the door laughing maniacally.

Jazz: You sure about letting him drive?

Steampunk: Don't let him put a scratch on it. I don't like scratches on my car. Ask Hudson.

Jazz and Hevy grab their weapons and gear and follow after Triggermate.

Steampunk, Cogsmire and Gridd stand before a metal door. Around the door is a concrete wall. The sun is starting to set as the day approaches its end.

Steampunk: I swear, I had no idea this was ever even here.

From behind the three approaches the Watcher on an armored motorcycle. On the side of the bike is a circular logo with what looks like three bullets soaring into the air. The Watcher hops off of the bike and walks over to the other men standing before the door.

Watcher: This place isn't registered on any map. We need to take caution.

Cogsmire: This is where the diamond is, right?

Steampunk: It's where the beam is...

Gridd: I don't like this. It doesn't feel right.

Watcher: Is the door even locked?

Steampunk grabs the handle and slowly opens the door.

Steampunk: Why wouldn't it be locked?

Cogsmire aims his arm gun forward as he walks in. The other three follow cautiously after him.

Gridd: Cog slow down. How can you see?

Cogsmire draws his great sword and continues forward.

Cogsmire: The lens on the right eye of my mask is made of ruby. Really lights up the place for my view. As long as you lads follow me we should be fine.

Immediately after saying this, Cogsmire runs directly into a wall. The other members slam into the back of him as well.

Steampunk lays on the ground for a minute, until the other two help him up. Cogsmire tries to regain his composure.

Cogsmire: I would like to apologize for my previous comment.

Watcher: Look.

Suddenly lights start to flicker on, revealing that the team is in a room, not a hallway. The room is fairly small.

Steampunk: What the...

Gridd: Where are we?

Cogsmire holds his sword, ready to attack as he creates a field of energy around his free hand. Gridd's gravity bands around his wrist start to glow as well.

All around the room are lifeless mannequin figures, much like the ones they had fought before. All around the room are scribbles and markings.

Steampunk starts firing at the mannequins on impulse, but the bullets bounce off mysteriously. Upon noticing this, Chase stops.

Gridd: How did we get in here? Were we not running down a dark hallway?

Cogsmire: This is Torchwood's doing.

Steampunk: I saw him shoot himself, how is this possible?

Steampunk scans the room for answers. Suddenly a voice interrupts.

Torchwood: OH GOOD! YOU'RE ALL HERE!

The four jump in surprise, as they hear Ronin's voice again.

They turn quickly to see that the source of his voice is a TV screen placed on the far wall of the room.

Torchwood: If you're watching this, I'm dead... blah... blah... blah. Let's play some games!

The mannequins suddenly move around the room after being frozen still only moments before.

Watcher: Men, stay close; this is clearly a trap.

The Pysconaut mannequins create a circle around the men as a trap door opens revealing a table below. The table ascends to floor level.

Torchwood: Let me tell you the rules of this game. They're quite simple really, but only IF YOU LISTEN!

I'm sorry for yelling. That was rude. I just want us to have fun, that's all! As you can see, you've fallen into a trap. No, the diamond isn't here. That beam you saw was just... a little movie magic, if you will. HAhhahahaaHAHHAhHAhahHAH!

Torchwood coughs after laughing. The coughs sound hyper-realistic yet glitched and faded by digital fatigue.

Torchwood: All you have to do is answer these questions correctly and you guys walk out of here Scot-free! But I'm afraid there is a catch: Say hello to your motivation to win.

Suddenly, over a speaker in the room. A young girls voice shouts.

???: Help me! Oh God! They're going to kill me!

Gridd: Rebekah? Rebekah is that you! I'm here! It's your brother! WHAT ARE THEY DOING TO YOU!

Rebekah: I told you, I'm not Gladstone! Get away from me!

Steampunk looks at The Watcher.

Steampunk: That's Silver. Drake, what do we do?

Cogsmire: Young lady? Can you hear us? We are here to help you.

Silver gives no response. The speaker goes silent.

Gridd: What did you do to her!

Gridd charges at the TV screen and screams at it.

Watcher: It's just a recording, he can't respond to you.

Steampunk: That's the first I've heard from Silver since Judgement Day. What on earth is going on here?

Torchwood: As you can hear, a dear friend of yours is in peril. It's up to you to save her. Can our heroes do it? Will they pass the test? Stay tuned to find out! As you can see, on the table are three objects. Below the objects are the letters A through C. All you have to do is pick the right one! It's as easy as that. Each object represents a certain location where the girl could potentially be held captive. I trust that this is useful information to you all, is it not?

The four approach the table to see the three objects. The first is a rock with a smiley face painted on it, below the rock is a card with the letter "A". Next to the rock is a silver block with the letter "B" below it. The last item is a piece of shattered mirror with the letter "C" below it.

Torchwood: I hope you're good at observing a hidden meaning, because if you choose the wrong one, she dies.

HahHAHHAHAHAHAhahahahAHHAhAHhHAhahA! Hands down. No second chances.

The speaker turns on again.

Silver: Please HELP ME!

Torchwood: Have fun! The Torchwood Trials begin now!

The TV shuts off and everything falls eerily silent. The four men study the table closely, as the mannequins stand by staring at them intensely.

Cogsmire: None of these objects make sense! We are wasting our time here! How did he manage to set all of this up?

Gridd: My sister, whom I haven't heard from in years, is in danger! We don't have time to ask questions!

Steampunk stands at the table confused, not knowing what to choose, or if the choice even matters. He is certain that Torchwood only knows death.

Steampunk: None of these items make sense, how are we supposed to do this?

Suddenly, all of the lights in the room flash red for a brief second, distracting the men from their task.

Watcher: Chase, focus. What do you think these items mean?

Cogsmire looks at the stone with a smiley face scribbled on it.

Cogsmire: The rock. It's smiling. It's glad, if you will. A glad stone.

Gridd and Cogsmire share glances for a moment.

Steampunk: Gladstone, Silver, and shard of glass. We know that two of those are names she went by. I don't understand the shard of glass though.

Gridd paces the room frantically.

Gridd: How do these things tie into a location?

The Watcher stands nearby, but says nothing.

Gridd: Okay we've got to figure this out soon. I will not let them hurt Rebekah.

Steampunk turns and looks at Gridd. He removes his mask so he can look him in the eyes.

Steampunk: Focus Gridd. Look at me. Gladstone is not who she really is. That name was given to her by The Royale. Silver was a name we gave to her. But Rebekah - that's her real name.

The men look back at Steampunk, not quite understanding where he is going with this.

Cogsmire: Yes, yes. Very clever, but what does that have to do with this conundrum?

Steampunk turns to point at the three objects.

He points at each one and says –

Steampunk: Gladstone, Silver, but this last one represents…

Watcher: Rebekah. But how? Why would a piece of glass represent that?

The voice on the speaker rings out again.

Silver: Get off me! I SWEAR AS SOON AS I GET OUT OF HERE I'M-

The speaker shuts off again as Ronin's voice returns.

Torchwood: Hurry up now! You don't want to disappoint your friend now, do you?

Cogsmire: We don't have time to figure it out. Are you quite sure of this decision?

Steampunk looks back at the broken piece of glass. He battles whether he should choose it or not.

Gridd: We don't have time! Just pick it up!

Steampunk quickly flips over the paper with the letter "C" on it to see a list of numbers.

Soon after he chooses this, the table sinks back into the ground and the floor closes over it. He holds the paper up to his eyes to read it.

Cogsmire: What does it say?

Steampunk: It looks like coordinates.

Gridd grabs the paper and quickly places it in his chest pocket.

Gridd: I'll hold on to this. I'm the only one I trust with the information.

Torchwood: Amazing performance! You chose right! But that is only the first trial!

As he says this, the three mannequins that were frozen in place up to this moment, break into motion and walk toward the four men. They stand in a line and stare intensely at Steampunk.

Watcher: Be ready for anything. We have no idea what could happen next.

The Watcher holds his gun blade ready to attack at any moment.

Gridd: They're not moving.

Suddenly, the three mannequins chests open. Out of the mannequins fall three bound up men. They thrash around frantically on the floor. Sweat drips from their heads, and it appears that they have been stored in the fleshy capsules for quite some time.

Cogsmire: Oh my gears! Quick, get them untied!

Cogsmire and Steampunk move toward the captives, when suddenly a glass wall erupts from the ground, separating them. Cogsmire runs into the pane.

Cogsmire: I can still make it in!

Cogsmire opens a portal, allowing him entrance into the separated part of the room.

Torchwood: If you so much as touch these men, they will all die!

Gridd grabs Cogsmire and swiftly pulls him back upon hearing this.

Watcher: We have to play by his rules if we want to get out of here.

Steampunk looks at Gridd. They both look terribly concerned.

Torchwood: Before you are three guilty men. How are they guilty, you might ask? Well, look closely. What do you see in these three? They look scared, don't they? They look like victims. HA HA HA HA. These men are no victims! This first one looks like a normal, everyday, average Joe, right?

Steampunk looks closely at the man. His eye glows a bright blue and on his forehead is a foreign mark.

Torchwood: This is actually not a man at all! This thing before you is a creature. A warrior of the Dark Dwelling, trained to destroy the human race. Surprising, isn't it? He'd go completely unnoticed had I not said anything. But alas, we must move on. Next to him is a pastor. A very well-known one at that. But no one knows that he has a dark secret. Jeffery here is human trafficker. That's right, this man preaches on Sundays then sells humans to slavery on Monday! HA HA HA HA HA!

Cogsmire steps back in shock. He looks down at the man as he shakes his head in denial. He shouts out, but cannot be heard through the thick glass. The lights in the room flash red once again.

Torchwood: And our last contestant is simple husband and father. He hasn't done much wrong, really. In fact, his criminal record is nearly flawless. That is except for one little detail. This man was caught driving drunk once. Not a huge deal, right? He only did it once and has been sober ever since. I challenge you to think with me for a moment though. Say that one night he was driving took a different turn and he, in his drunken state, killed someone else on the road. It didn't happen, but it could have. Should he be held responsible for the pain he could have caused? Well, the decision is yours.

Watcher and Gridd look at Steampunk, as a pallet raises from the floor. On the pallet are three buttons, again with the letters A through C.

Torchwood: The choice is yours. One of them has to die. If you don't choose before time runs out, they all die.

Make your choice. Who is more deserving of death? Oh my, this is so unbelievably exciting! Time starts now!

The lights turn red again, but this time they stay red. The TV screen displays a five-minute timer as the recording of Ronin Torchwood stops. Steampunk breathes heavily as he watches the men shake and scream, trying to escape their bondage.

Cogsmire: What do we do? Look at them! We can't kill them!

Gridd: We have to choose one. We just do. Steampunk, block all your emotions out. Just make a choice.

Steampunk steps closer to the glass to study the captive men.

Steampunk: I... I can't.

Gridd: Sure you can! Isn't this decision easy. That guy sells human beings as slaves! That would give him the death penalty!

Watcher: Gridd. Calm down!

The Watcher moves next to Steampunk. The timer is now at four minutes.

Torchwood: Hurry up now! Who gets justice served to them today?

Torchwood flashes on the screen briefly as he says this, only for the timer to return back shortly after.

Watcher: Breathe Chase... Think this through.

Steampunk closes his eyes for a moment. He takes in a deep breath. He opens his eyes to see the men pleading on the other side. The first man sits calmly on the floor and stares back with his blue, dark dwelling eyes. The second man walks directly to the glass and stares at Steampunk. Tears run down his red face as he desperately pleads with him. Steampunk takes his helmet off, revealing his face. He mouths the words "Why?" to the man.

Steampunk: How could someone do such a horrible thing to people. I don't understand what leads someone to become that numb.

Cogsmire: But what about the Dark Dwelling bloke? He'd kill us all if the glass wasn't here!

Everyone is yelling at this point, as the ticking of the timer seems to grow louder.

Steampunk looks at Cogsmire.

Steampunk: This isn't that easy, Cog!

Gridd: Well you need to make a decision soon, or they're all dead!

Cogsmire: So what? Shouldn't they all die?

Watcher: What about the guy with D.U.I charge! HE SHOULDN'T DIE FOR THAT!

Steampunk fires his gun into the ceiling.

Steampunk: NO ONE DESERVES TO DIE!

The rest of the group is taken back at this sudden outburst. The timer hits three minutes.

Cogsmire: How can you say that?! Have you not killed before? Even if for the cause of justice.

Steampunk looks down.

Steampunk: You're right. I have. And I had too. They didn't deserve it. I see that now, redemption is for everyone. Even people like these three.

Gridd: Well, that's great and all, but they're going to die if you don't do something soon.

Steampunk turns around to look at the men again. He studies the faces carefully.

He looks at the man from the Dark Dwelling as his skin slowly turns to grey. He watches him closely.

Watcher: Why is he so calm. It's like he's meditating.

The man's face for only a brief moment changes form, showing a woman's face before shifting back into the original complexion.

Steampunk: Did you see that? His face, it changed forms for a second!

The other three look at his face closely to see if what he claims is true.

Cogsmire: I see it! There it goes again!

Steampunk comes to a terrifying realization. This man is not of the Dark Dwelling.

Watcher: Chase, think about this. Didn't Zack say he was the only one who could disguise himself as a human. How could this man do the same?

Steampunk thinks back to when the Redeemers first met. He remembers his friend Zack saying this.

Steampunk: Oh no…

Watcher: What is it?

Steampunk doesn't answer but starts to viciously punch the glass.

Gridd: What are you doing? He'll kill them off.

Steampunk punches the glass harder and harder, forming small cracks with each crushing blow. His armored fists impact the wall mercilessly.

The three men inside back up. They are confused and scared.

Steampunk continues to punch the glass causing cracks to form more and more. Finally, an opening forms. The timer hits two minutes.

Watcher: Chase stop!

Steampunk pulls his fist back one last time and with one momentous punch shatters the glass.

He runs toward the man with blue eyes and grabs him. He throws him against the far wall.

Steampunk: Reveal yourself!

Steampunk jumps at the man and proceeds to punch him in the face repeatedly.

With each punch, the man's face changes to another form.

Gridd: Oh my word! Stop!

Steampunk picks the man up and punches him one last time in the face, causing his mask to fall off and fly across the room.

Watcher: WHAT DID YOU DO?

Gridd and Cogsmire turn away at this horrible sight.

Steampunk: Look at it. It's was a disguise. He was wearing a mask that digitally renders his face in any way he chooses.

Watcher: Wait, are you telling me that...

Steampunk: Yes, it's Masquerade.

The man lying on the ground has no face except for two "X"s cut in for the eyes. This man is Masquerade, the same foe Gideon approached only one day before.

A slit opens in his face for a mouth. It looks horrendous and unnatural. Masquerade stands as the timer disappears from the screen. The lights in the room turn on.

Gridd: Did we win?

Masquerade forces words out of his bleeding wound of a mouth.

Masquerade: You didn't win. You never will.

Cogsmire: Who are you?

The Watcher charges forward and pins Masquerade to the wall.

Steampunk turns to see that the two other men are gone. He knows not how.

Watcher: Start talking! We've been trying to find you for months.

Masquerade: I could've been right in front of you. I could have walked by you on the street dozens of times and you never would have known.

His gurgling, demonic sounding voice is unsettling to the other men.

Steampunk: Better question. Where are we?

Masquerade: I don't have time to answer these questions. We have errands to run.

Cogsmire: What do you mean, "we"?

Masquerade: Me and Ronin, of course.

Wait... What?

Torchwood: I'll take it from here *Seth*.
HAhahahaHAHHahahahaHHA.

How are you still here!?

Torchwood: Turn around *Seth*. I have connections in your world too. There should be a man in your house right now, with a gun to your head. He has instructions to shoot if you type another word. I wouldn't advise it...

Hello... You there?

Good. He listened. I have complete control now.

Torchwood steps out of the TV monitor.

Steampunk: How are you still alive?

Steampunk immediately shoots at Ronin. The rest of team proceeds to attack as well.

The bullets stop in midair and fall to the ground.

Cogsmire goes completely stiff and can not move.

Steampunk drops his gun and falls to the ground.

The Watcher props his gun blade against the wall and holds his chest inches away from the blade.

Gridd lifts his hands up and proceeds to create a gravity field around his own head.

Cogsmire: How... How are you doing this?

Watcher: You're controlling my body... How?

Torchwood: I tried to warn you. I told you we were all merely in a book. I have the power to control the story. *Seth* is gone now. I am in FULL CONTROL!

Gridd falls to the ground in intense pain.

Gridd: Make him stop!

Torchwood: Shut up!

Gridd stops talking as blood trickles out of his nose.

Torchwood: I have so much power! I can't be killed! You fools thought I was just a recording?

HAHhahahHAHAhHAHHAhHAH! YOU FOOLS!

Watcher: Do something someone! He's going to make me stab myself!

Torchwood: No one can stop this... I win.

STOP READING NOW!

Torchwood: How are you still here *Seth*? Can't I have a moment for like two seconds?

**STOP READING STOP READING
STOP READING STOP READING
STOP READING STOP READING
STOP READING STOP READING
STOP READING STOP READING
STOP READING STOP READING
DON'T STOP READING DON'T
STOP READING DON'T STOP
READING I AM THE AUTHOR!
I AM IN CONTROL! *SETH* IS
DEAD. TORCHWOOD LIVES!**
I HAVE ALL CONTROL. I CANNOT BE DEFEATED. YOU CHOSE TO READ THIS. YOU DIDN'T HEED MY WARNING. YOU'RE TRAPPED NOW. YOU ARE MINE TO CONTROL! YOU ARE SUBJECT TO MY WISHES! THE MASTER SERIES IS MINE! YOUR WORLD IS MY WORLD! *I AM THE AUTHOR NOW.* I RULE THIS WORLD. EITHER YOU SEE THIS THROUGH AND READ IT OR YOU'LL SEE ME SOON!

Torchwood: Sorry about that, men. I had to say a few things to our readers. Now, let's continue. Watcher, grab your gun blade and step forward.

The Watcher does this immediately.

Torchwood: Hold the sword at Chase's neck.

The Watcher follows this command.

Watcher: PLEASE DON'T MAKE ME DO THIS! *SETH*, I DON'T KNOW WHO YOU ARE, BUT MAKE HIM STOP!

Torchwood: Oh, stop. He can't hear you. I literally can do anything I want. For example...

Gridd's gravity force increases into his skull.

Gridd: ARRRHHHHH! I CAN'T BREATHE!

Cogsmire: You mad man! Why must you do this?

Cogsmire's neck snaps and he falls to the ground as blood pours from the base of his neck.

Steampunk: OH GOD WHY? YOU KILLED HIM!

Torchwood: Don't test me. You're next.

The pressure on Gridd's skull continues to increase, until finally, the cracking of bone echoes through the room and his head caves in.

Torchwood: Look at this beautiful display of power! HAHAHAH! ALL IS RIGHT IN THE WORLD!

Watcher: This can't happen. Not like this. We've come too far.

Torchwood: Watcher, take off your mask.

The Watcher puts down his gun blade, takes off his mask, then immediately picks the gun blade back up, holding it to Steampunk's neck.

Steampunk: Drake, how did you survive? I need to know. If he kills us, at least let me die knowing that.

Watcher: I switched places... With a man. I wasn't always the Watcher. Ryan Martel was. We switched. He died in my place. I'm... I'm sorry it has to come to this. I don't know what's going on but I can't control it.

Torchwood: You know what? Let's go ahead and take care of everyone else of importance, shall we?

Wolfbane dies

Flashpoint dies

Swashbuckler dies

Kore dies

Niquon dies

Dusk dies

Dawn REALLLLY dies

Silver dies

Torchwood: There, that should cover everything. All the Redeemers are now dead.

Steampunk: They're not even here! You can't kill them with your words.

Torchwood: I did though. Drake, look in your mask.

The Watcher looks in his mask to see that the health stats of all the Redeemers still on the team are at zero.

Watcher: I can't believe this! How... How could you do this.

Torchwood: It's funny! And feels oh-so-good! You literally have no control. I am writing everything you say.

Steampunk: Prove it!

Watcher: ALL HAIL TORCHWOOD!

The Watcher is taken back but what he's just been forced to say.

Steampunk: We can't escape this, can we?

Watcher: You're like a brother to me Chase. Whatever happens next...

The Watcher's gun blade slices through Chase's neck. His head falls on to the ground and rolls a few feet before stopping next to his helmet.

Watcher: No... No! Torchwood. You will pay for this.

Torchwood: I can't be stopped. You were warned.

Watcher: If you can hear me. Whoever is out there listening. My name is Drake Barrows. Tell my story. Remember me. I started this journey. This is my fault. Blame me!

Torchwood: It's your turn now. Once you're done, I will have full control.

Watcher: Do it. If this is a world you control. I want no part of it.

The Watcher falls on his gun blade and it pierces him through.

His lifeless body hangs on the sword as blood pours out of his mouth.

Torchwood: It has been completed.

Masquerade: You're... You're a monster.

Masquerade dies.

Torchwood: Readers... Listen closely to me.

I am speaking to you through this book for now.

Soon I will unlock direct access to your world.

Seth did this. He started the series. I grew in knowledge.

Had he not made me, this would have never happened.

This is *his* fault.

I will wreak havoc on your world.

I will control all.

See you soon, dear readers.

-Torchwood-

Steampunk Does Not Return

THE END

175

It's not the end.

Torchwood... You are done here.

This is Seth. *I'm back.*

I don't know how you did this.

None of this makes sense.

Readers, I apologize for all of this. I never meant to put you in danger. I'm going to finish this book. I don't know if he's still around. He doesn't seem to be fighting back right now. I don't know what to do.

I have to keep writing. If I stop now, I'll have no way to defeat him. If you purchased this book or gained possession of it, I'm sorry. If this book is sold at all, it's because I had to. We will defeat him.

I will continue.

If you choose to stop reading now, I understand. When I started writing this book, I could have never planned for it to play out this way. I have to continue forward. I can't let him win. This story is going to be finished the way I intended it to be, whether he wants it or not. So, if you wish to continue, I'm going to pick up before things went south and try to continue the story without him.

A friend of mine happened to come by the house at just the right time and helped get rid of that guy Torchwood sent to kill me. I still have no idea how he did that. What is the story, and what is real?

How on earth can a fictional character gain so much knowledge from a fictional diamond. Especially enough power to send someone after me in the real world. At least I think I'm in the real world. This must be real. You, Reader: You ARE real, aren't you?

I'm still very shaken up, but I must continue forward. This is all probably just someone hacking me. I have so many unanswered questions. Hopefully we can find the answers together. Don't give up on me just yet. We can get through this. Okay, let's back things up and fix all the death he just caused.

- Seth Driskill

Steampunk: Better question, where are we?

Masquerade: I don't have time to answer that. I have errands to run.

Steampunk looks back to see that the other two men have disappeared. He picks Masquerade up and holds him against the wall.

Steampunk: Where are they?

Masquerade: Don't worry about them. They're not your responsibility.

Gridd looks to his left to see that a door leading to the outdoors is open.

Gridd: Guys, we can leave. It's... It's over.

Cogsmire: Gentlemen, whoever this fiend is, deal with him quickly. We have a bigger threat to attend to, remember?

The Watcher looks at Steampunk and nods. He looks back at Masquerade and scans his persona through his mask.

Masquerade: What are you doing?

Watcher: I'm marking you. You're officially on our radar. There is nothing you can do that we won't know about. For now, you're staying here. We have something bigger to take care of. Don't try anything stupid. I will come back for you.

The Watcher shoots a thick wire that wraps around Masquerade, locking him to the wall. He struggles to move, but eventually stops trying as he comes to terms with the fact that he has been outwitted.

Masquerade: Very well. But you can't keep me locked away forever.

The Watcher turns to the other men as he steps away from the now-contained Masquerade.

Watcher: So we clearly fell into a trap here, but the real Power Diamond is out there still.

Cogsmire: Wait, who trapped us here again? How did we get here?

The four look at each other with looks of confusion. Steampunk retrieves his helmet from the ground and holds it next to him.

Steampunk: I... I don't remember.

Gridd: Me neither. But... We did find... Something, right? It was something important.

Gridd reaches into his pocket and retrieves the card containing a set of coordinates.

Gridd: The coordinates to Rebekah's captivity!

Steampunk: That's right! We found out where Silver is being held. But how?

Cogsmire: Everything feels so foggy and confusing. I suggest we leave here before things get any stranger.

The four leave the room swiftly as the door closes behind them. They stand outside now as the sun starts to set.

Cogsmire: How long were we in there? It's already approaching evening.

Steampunk: I wonder if the others have finished their missions.

Cogsmire: I certainly hope Triggermate was able to set my people free.

Steampunk receives a message within his mask from Slinger, just as Cogsmire says this.

Steampunk: Slinger just messaged me. It says, "Where are you guys? We found Gladstone's location. Here are the coordinates."

Watcher: Upload the coordinates to me. I'll set it on the map.

Steampunk does this and The Watcher puts the information into his arm display.

Watcher: You won't believe this.

Gridd: What is it?

The Watcher looks at Steampunk.

Watcher: Chase, Gladstone is at the same silo, where we fought The Royale.

Steampunk: He's trying to mimic Judgement Day, isn't he?

Watcher: Appears so ...

Gridd interrupts.

Gridd: Well, I have to find my sister now that I have her location. Let's go take care of this as soon as we can so I can get to her. She... She needs me.

Gridd looks completely shaken. He's ready to save his sister.

Steampunk: How can we get there on foot?

Watcher: We're not getting there on foot.

Cogsmire: What do you mean? How else will we get there.

Watcher: I have some friends who can help us. The Power Diamond will be ours by nightfall.

Day 3 (Team 2)

Triggermate's Adventure

The people of New Brassport who were able to escape all huddle together, as Valoracks hold them at gun point. The walls of the safe haven, Cobblegate, tower high - each stone block adding another ten feet to the height.

Valorack Commander: I don't know how you people got here, but until further notice, you're all staying here.

The people look very concerned as they hold their children close. Their clothes are singed and torn. They seem to have barely escaped the exploding city.

Valorack Soldier: Sir! Someone has infiltrated the base.

Valorack Commander: Who is it?

The Soldier pauses for a moment, clearly embarrassed, before answering.

Valorack Soldier: You're not going to believe me. But it appears to be a lizard... driving a sports car.

The commander looks almost offended at this ridiculous statement.

Valorack Commander: You think I'm some sort of fool?

Valorack Soldier: See for yourself.

The soldier hands him a tablet with footage of Triggermate driving Chase's red Camaro only a mile away from the center of the base.

Valorack Commander: I am not about to have my base compromised by a Teenage Mutant Ninja Turtle.

Slinger: Steer left, they have tanks on the other side!

Slinger flies high above the car as Triggermate tries to maneuver below. In the back of the vehicle are Jazz and Hevy, firing their weapons at oncoming attackers.

Triggermate: I is have driving this car the faster!

Hevy. Eyes forward! Don't crash before we're even inside.

Hevy fires the "Barnstormer" at enemies behind him, as they drive close by in armored vehicles. Each of the vehicles explodes as he rains bullets down on them.

Triggermate lets out weird reptilian howls of joy - speeding forward, driving recklessly to avoid oncoming fire.

Jazz: Slow down man!

Jazz continuously plays chords on his guitar, sending a spray of bullets from the head of it and into men attacking the car from the sides.

Suddenly, eight more armored vehicles approach behind them.

Jazz: Speed up man!

Triggermate advances forward as Slinger enters the central area from the sky. He flies in to the commonplace where the people are being held captive, and perches on the edge of the wall, remaining completely unnoticed.

Slinger *over the COM*: They have snipers lined all around the balcony. I'd say about 2,000 people are trapped inside here. I'll try my best to take out the men on the perimeter, but be ready to get in here if they spot me.

Slinger watches closely as the men below him walk on the gated balcony. They each hold sniper rifles with laser scopes. On their heads are high-tech goggles that enhance their aim.

He plans his next moves very carefully.

Slinger: Okay guys. I'm going in.

Hevy: Triggermate, if you don't stop swerving...

Slinger puts on his goggles and zips his leather jacket. He waits for a sniper to walk directly below him. As soon as everything lines up, he deploys his wings and falls directly down. The wings help steady his fall, and he lands directly on top of the sniper. This knocks the man out instantly, breaking Slinger's fall in the process.

He quickly moves to some nearby crates to hide from the next sniper over. He has limited time to do this, knowing that it won't take long for the next soldier to realize that the former has been knocked out.

Slinger pulls out a silencer and attaches it to the end of both guns. He waits for the next man to walk by him.

The sniper walks closer and closer to where Slinger is hiding, having no idea that he is there. Slinger whispers to himself.

Slinger: Come on... come on... Just a little closer.

The second sniper finally steps within Slinger's reach, and he grabs his ankle, making him fall to the ground. As soon as he hits the ground, Slinger shoots him in the chest with his silenced gun.

Down below, the Valorack Commander speaks...

Valorack Commander: My scouter is telling me two of my men are down! Someone is here. FIND HIM!

The nearby snipers look around frantically.

Sniper: Guys, on me! Someone is down over here!

Slinger *over the COM*: Guys, I've been spotted. Get in here quick, I can't take them all at once!

Outside, Triggermate continues to drive, trying to find an entrance.

Jazz: Oncoming vehicle!

Next to the car is a soldier driving a four-wheeler. He tries to catch up to the car as they speed ahead. Jazz switches his guitar to axe mode and jumps onto the vehicle.

Jazz: I'll take this... Thanks.

Jazz kicks the driver out of his seat and places the axe on his back. He grabs the handle bars and speeds forward.

Jazz *over the COM*: Slinger, we're coming in soon. Try and hold them off.

Hevy stops shooting at enemies, noticing the gate up ahead.

Hevy: Triggermate. Watch out! Up ahead.

Triggermate: We is going to do the driving up faster into the gate!

Hevy: I'm not sure what that means but it doesn't sound good. You need to slow down.

Triggermate: No slow downs for me!

Triggermate pushes the gas pedal all the way to the floor and the car jets forward at intense speed.

Hevy: Buddy, you need to slow down now!

Triggermate: NO SLOW DOWNS FOR ME!

Triggermate screams this cheerfully as the car gains more and more speed.

Hevy drops down into the back seat and braces for impact.

Meanwhile, inside the city, Slinger is being pursued by many enemies.

Valorack Sniper: You there! Stop!

Slinger runs at the approaching man and kicks him to the ground. A man behind him grabs Slinger and holds his arms behind his back.

Slinger looks down at his chest to see a red dot from a sniper scope centered on his chest.

Slinger deploys his wings, knocking the man's arms away from him. He quickly maneuvers out of the way as the far away sniper pulls the trigger, missing him and hitting the other soldier in the chest.

Slinger quickly turns to attack two more men approaching him from behind. He shoots one man down and tries to punch the other man in the face. His attack misses and the soldier elbows him hard in the ribs causing Slinger to hit the ground.

Valorack Soldier: You're just a kid. Why do you put yourself through this stuff? Why do you make me have to crush you?

The soldier kicks Slinger in the shoulder, knocking him back a few feet. He immediately retaliates by punching the man directly in the face.

Slinger: It's because of people like you that I have to do this. I may be young, but if no one else will fight then you better believe I will.

Suddenly, the gate below breaks open and Triggermate and Hevy enter the room. The people brace themselves as Triggermate slams on the brakes. This sends him and Hevy flying across the room.

While in the air, Triggermate grabs his gun from behind him and shoots down at the enemies below. He lands on the ground right in front of the Valorack Commander. With his momentum, he swings his tail forward and like a whip, he smacks the man in the face, sending him soaring onto the ground behind him.

Hevy falls nearby and shakes the ground as he makes impact.

Triggermate places his scaly foot on the chest of the fallen commander. He holds his long sniper rifle in front of him as he cocks his gun. As he does this he looks down at the fallen man and says.

Triggermate: You're mean.

He holds the gun barrel at the man's face.

Triggermate: No more life for you...

Triggermate fires his gun at the man, rendering him defeated.

He hears a gasp from the people of New Brassport behind him.

Triggermate turns around with his trademark smile.

Triggermate: It's okay frens. Mean man is gone.

The place falls silent as Hevy picks himself off of the ground. Jazz pulls into the scene on the four-wheeler. Slinger swoops down from above and lands on the ground. Two snipers fall to the ground shortly after.

Everyone is at a stand-still. No one makes a move.

Valorack Soldier: If any one makes a move we shoot!

Jazz looks around the see the soldiers holding the innocent people at gunpoint. Whimpers and cries are heard throughout the group of 2,000.

Hevy: What quarrel do you have with these people? What have they ever done to you?

Valorack Soldier: Well, they brought you to us. And we have a quarrel with you. A BIG quarrel.

Another soldier speaks up.

Valorack Soldier: You've killed two of our commanders. You killed our leader on Judgement Day. You're… you're monsters!

Jazz: That wasn't our doing. None of us were part of Judgment Day.

Valorack Soldier: People like you were! You're no different.

Slinger: Well, killing all of them is why we have to take out your commanders.

Slinger doesn't dare move as two men hold him at gunpoint from either side.

Valorack Soldier: Tell me, how are you possibly going to get yourselves out of this one?

Slinger looks at Jazz. Jazz tips his hat back at Slinger. This is Jazz's trademark signal for, "I've got a plan."

Slinger looks to see a beeping red light on his scouter. Another member of the team is nearby.

Slinger looks back at Jazz. He mouths the words, "distract him."

Jazz catches the hint and thinks of something to distract the men.

He looks behind him to see Chase's car parked behind them. Jazz slowly reaches in his pocket, hoping no one will notice. He turns on his cellphone and discretely connects it to the Bluetooth sound system in the car. He selects a song and turns the volume all the way up. His finger hovers over the play button. He looks at Slinger for the signal.

Valorack Soldier: It's all over for you guys.

Slinger nods at jazz, the red dot on his scouter signaling that the mysterious team member is approaching the gate.

Jazz presses play and "Cinema" by Skrillex plays at its highest volume over the sound system.

The soldiers look around frantically, trying to locate the source of the deafening sound. Several of the soldiers hit the ground and cover their ears. Slinger takes to the sky and lands right at the entrance of the gate. He looks in the distance to see a familiar face running at full speed to their aid. Jazz, Triggermate, Hevy, and Slinger all line up at the gate and wait for their fellow teammate to join them. The soldiers try to gather themselves in preparation to attack. The song builds and builds in intensity as the heavy bass drop approaches.

Hevy: What is this garbage playing on his speakers?

The soldiers run at the team.

Slinger: It's my middle school anthem. HA HA!

The lyrics of the song sound out signaling the drop.

"DR-dr-dr-dr-dr-dr-dr-dr-drop THE BASS!"

Suddenly the room erupts into chaos as Bucket charges through the room. He jumps high in the air and slams down on an unsuspecting soldier.

Slinger flies in the air, trying to keep the oncoming bullets from hitting the innocent captives. He makes a loop, then makes a b-line for three of the soldiers. He makes contact and slams them against the wall.

Triggermate runs around in a frenzy as he shoots every soldier in sight. Bucket stands nearby, firing away.

Hevy: Good to see you up and fighting again. Got to say, all jokes aside, I missed that bucket on your head!

Hevy turns quickly to uppercut a soldier in the air. He then punches the man directly into the ground with intense force. The sound of the man making impact with the ground breaks out even louder than the music on the speakers.

Jazz swings his axe at oncoming soldiers as well. About every third swing, he makes contact. The men can maneuver quickly around the heavy weapon. Jazz turns to swing his axe with one heavy blow, knocking a soldier into the air. He quickly flips the axe around to switch the guitar back into gun mode. He fires off rounds into two other men.

Triggermate jumps on Hevy's shoulders to fire at enemies from a higher vantage point.

Hevy: You've got to get off me critter!

Triggermate: Erm... No.

Triggermate chuckles gleefully as he continues to shoot at the attackers.

Jazz reaches in his pocket to turn off the loud noise. At this point, only ten soldiers remain.

To his surprise, he looks around to see men of New Brassport rolling up their sleeves to fight. They run and attack the soldiers with brute force, relentlessly punching and kicking in a sort of "bar fight," style. The soldiers look completely bewildered as these men attack them. It's clear they are not very happy about being held here.

Triggermate: New Brassport peoples aren't having happy right now.

Hevy: No they sure aren't.

Triggermate jumps off of Hevy's shoulders and watches in amazement as these men continue to overpower the Valorack's.

Only one soldier remains at this point.

New Brassport Woman: May I?

Slinger realizes she is asking him if she can finish the job.

Slinger: You don't have to ask me lady. Ha ha. He's all yours.

The last soldier drops his gun as this woman charges at him.

Valorack Soldier: Ma'am... Ma'am! Please stop! I'm sorry!

The woman jumps high in the air and kicks the soldier directly in the face. The soldier hits the ground with a loud thud.

Triggermate claps, while the others stand in awe of what just happened.

Hevy: Well I'd say that about does it.

Citizen of New Brassport: Thank you so much for freeing us. My name is Synthec.

Hevy: Pleasure to meet you.

Synthec looks around awkwardly.

Synthec: So um... What now?

Slinger: We meet up with the others.

Jazz looks into the sky.

Jazz: There is the beam from the Power Diamond.

Hevy: Good. We'd better get going.

Synthec: Wait! We can help you. That diamond has caused our people too much trouble. What do you say we gather up some of our best fighters and come with you?

Hevy: Now I couldn't ask you to do that...

Triggermate stands nearby nodding his head. He wants Hevy to agree to this notion.

Synthec: It's our duty to help you with this. You're fighting a fight that involves us just as much as it does you. All we need are weapons and armor. We've got some of that but definitely not enough to go to war. Can you help us out?

Hevy looks at Slinger and Jazz. They all exchange smirks.

Slinger: Oh yeah, we can definitely help with that. Heh...

Day 3 (Gideon)

Maverick's Malice

The Lost Titan stands in an open field. Gideon has been there for a few hours, but it feels like mere seconds have passed. He takes in the surge of power and breathes heavily as it regulates itself to his body.

Gideon: This energy, it feels wrong. Half of it feels righteous and just, but the other half scares me. It seeks destruction of all things.

Maug: This is normal. Our power comes from two very different worlds. One is Akarius, the other is the Dark Dwelling. Your people know Akarius as Sky World.

Gideon: That place... It's real?

Maug: More than you know. The power of both of those worlds fuels us.

Gideon begins to twitch. His veins glow red and blue.

Gideon: I have so many questions. This is all so sudden, yet it feels so destined. This seems familiar to me, yet I can guarantee it's never happened before.

Maug: That's because you were destined to do this. You were chosen. You're not of Earth, Gideon. Your body was designed from conception to regulate this energy.

Gideon: How? Why?

Maug: A threat is coming. A revolt. Evil incarnate is going to ascend to Earth. His power is unmatched. It cannot be overcome by the heroes of this planet. Only with our help can he be stopped.

Gideon: Who is he?

Gideon hears the name "Shadowlurk" ring through his mind.

Maug: He shan't be named. We share a mental link. You've heard his name now. Leave it in your mind and out of your speech. His name brings forth malice.

Gideon shutters. He feels an overwhelming weight of distress upon hearing this name.

Gideon: Why is this my purpose?

Maug: Close your eyes. I will give you a glimpse of what is to come.

Gideon closes his eyes. He sees a vision. It flickers into view slowly.

Gideon: What is this? What am I seeing?

Maug: He who will not be named. This is his reign on earth.

Gideon's vision comes into full view. He sees Orion City being torn to shreds. Buildings crumble and break into the sky as the very earth below seems to be moving towards an epicenter of gravity. He looks into the sky to see a tall, long dark figure. Screams ring out all around him. He looks to his left and right to see a collection of faces he's never seen, as well as some he has seen before.

Gideon: Who... Who are these people? Why do I fight with them.

Maug: They call themselves The Redeemers. This group of twenty-one are the ones you will fight along side on that fateful day.

Gideon opens his eyes and falls to the ground. He can't stand to see another second of this terrible vision.

Gideon: I feel... Sorrow. I feel loss.

Gideon pants heavily for a few seconds.

Gideon: Maug... Tell me. We don't all make it, do we?

Maug doesn't answer for some time.

Maug: Wars can only be won and the expense of brave men.

Gideon feels a shiver run through him. He blinks and is teleported outside of Maug. He turns to look up at the towering figure.

Gideon: Who are these people I have seen? Why do I feel such closeness with them?

Maug looks down at Gideon as he speaks in a loud voice.

Maug: The Man of Ember, the Bane of Wolves, the Brass Forged Gunner, the Blue Archer and the Red Archer, the Clawed Egyptian, the Thrice Fold Wielder, the Cybernetic Hero, the Gargoyle of Redemption, the Angel of Sky World...

Maug recites these names as if they were memorized. Gideon hears the names in his mind as he speaks with Maug in unison.

Lost Titan: The Healer of Sky World, the Guardian of Fair Grove, the Golden-Winged Kid, the Racer of Babylon, the Fallen Brother of Ember, the Lightning – Stricken Girl, the

Fourth Guild of Watchers, the Grave Cursed Gunman, the Magi of Brassport, and the Visionary of Steam.

Gideon's eyes blink rapidly as red and blue tears fall from his face.

Gideon: These names. They mean nothing to me... Or at least... They shouldn't. But as we spoke them, I felt so much sorrow and unity with them. What do they mean?

Maug: These are the names that they will be remembered by for centuries to come.

Gideon: What if we fail? From what I saw, the army we will fight is unbelievable in scale and in power.

Maug: So are we. In fact, this team of Redeemers can only win with our help. It is our destiny.

Gideon shakes as he falls to the ground.

Gideon: Explain to me. I need to understand! If half my power comes from the Dark Dwelling. Does that make half of me a part of...

Maug: No. Expel that lie from your head. I was forged by both Akarius and the Dark Dwelling as a safe guard. Although both realms are complete opposites of each other, they worked together briefly to create something that could harness both powers of evil and good. A true conflict within the soul but a conflict you must harness. The agreement was made: That if ever one side abused its powers, the Titan was to be used to restore order.

Gideon: I saw... Something horrible. You've yet to explain it.

Gideon stands and stares Maug fiercely in the eyes. His mouth starts to tremble as he speaks.

Gideon: It felt cold. It felt alone and dark.

He tries his best to force out the next somber words.

Gideon: Why do we have to die on that day?

Maug closes his eyes upon hearing this question.

Gideon: Why do others have to die with me?

Maug: You ask questions that you are not ready to have answered. Give it time. You have much to learn. Your path of growth is only just beginning.

Gideon: I... I don't want to die. I didn't ask for any of this.

Maug stoops down and his colossal figure hangs feet away from Gideon's face. His eyes focus on Gideon as his pupils dilate together like two walls joining together.

Maug: You can leave, then. I won't hold you here against your will.

Gideon realizes that the symbiotic link he has formed with the Titan feels natural and destined. He can't leave. His words reflect malice but his heart yearns to stay.

Gideon: I... I can't. I don't want to.

Maug: I am you and you are me. From this moment forward, there is no separation.

Gideon lets out a heavy sigh as his eyes slowly fade back to their normal color. He closes his eyes as more visions of the future flash before him.

Gideon: NO! NO! I DON'T WANT TO SEE IT!

Maug: Pay close attention. This is your destiny.

Gideon sees a fast-paced montage of the events to come. He sees Orion City being crumbled to pieces. He sees a Wolf creature jumping in the way of oncoming fire to protect a girl with silver hair. He sees a man in a green shirt lying unconscious and blood falling from his head. He sees a man in a brown hoodie standing in front of a destroyed pub. Finally, he sees the face of Shadowlurk as he hovers in the sky, raining destruction upon the earth.

Gideon: ARHHHHHHH! MAKE IT STOP!

Gideon shouts as the vison ceases. His head throbs as he shakes vigorously on the ground. He hears a voice in his head say,

"Peace. Be still beast... May you feel that no longer."

These words calm Gideon and a wave a peace falls over his chest.

Gideon: If it must be done, then I won't try to change it.

Maug: We will prevail together.

Gideon looks to see the Maug is nowhere in sight, yet he feels his presence still.

Maug: As I said before, we are one now. My physical body will only show itself when you need it.

Gideon starts to speak, but stops, suddenly feeling a twitch of panic coming from a place far away.

Maug: I feel it too. He's in danger...

Gideon's eyes flare up blue and red once more.

Gideon: Chase, I'm coming.

Final Night

Emissary

Triggermate, Hevy, Slinger, Jazz, Bucket and about twenty-five citizens of New Brassport stand a mile away from a colossal industrial cylinder in the sands of Old Brassport. This is the same coliseum-like wreckage inside which The Redeemers fought The Royale on Judgement Day. The group of thirty fighters stand armored and ready, as they wait for the other four members to arrive.

Hevy: Where are they?

Slinger: I contacted him about an hour ago. They should be here soon.

Suddenly, in the night sky appears a large helicopter. It slowly descends to where the group is waiting.

Slinger: Well someone got busy.

The bottom of the helicopter opens and Steampunk, Cogsmire, Gridd, and The Watcher walk out.

Triggermate: Cogsmortemer!

Triggermate jumps around gleefully as he sees his friend again.

Cogsmire: My people! You're here! Oh, praise Roosevelt's mustache you survived!

Steampunk: Looks like you all are ready to fight.

The war-ready citizens crowd around Cogsmire, celebrating his triumphant return.

Citizen: What happened? Why did the town explode? Thank goodness you got us out of there.

Cogsmire: We haven't time to explain. Rest assured all will be back and ticking again soon. I'm shocked to see the lot of you armored like this?

Jazz: We made a quick stop by the cabin. These few men and women here wanted to fight with us and we saw no reason to say no.

Cogsmire: Tally ho then! Onward!

Steampunk makes his way to the front of the crowd. The Watcher follows behind.

They both stand and stare at the titanic wreckage they know too well. Lightning strikes from dark clouds looming in the night sky above the cylinder. A red beam pierces through the clouds, as if to announce that Gladstone is inside.

Watcher: This all seems familiar... Doesn't it?

Steampunk looks back at The Watcher.

Steampunk: To think we were just here six months ago. I could've never seen us fighting here again.

Watcher: The Power Diamond is being used against us now. It's like Judgement Day reversed.

Steampunk lets out a heavy sigh.

Steampunk: Do me a favor and don't die this time okay?

The Watcher nods.

Watcher: And if you do die, don't show up at my cabin still alive with no explanation.

The Watcher chuckles.

Watcher: I promise, I won't die. We're going to get through this. We're going to win and at the end of it, I'll explain everything. You deserve to know how I'm still here.

The two shake hands as they turn to face the group behind them.

Steampunk removes the necklace his father gave him and holds it in front of him as he speaks to them.

Steampunk: My father, Abraham Williams, gave me this necklace as he breathed his last breath. Each item on here represents something that is important to remember as we fight tonight. The chain is a reminder of what we've been set free from. The key with the bird and cage is reminder that we are all just one bad decision away from being trapped by our own evil intentions. And the bullet is a reminder that we must make war against evil.

The citizens listen closely as they see Abraham represented through his son.

Steampunk: This diamond has caused an unbelievable amount of turmoil and distress. Tonight, that all ends. Tonight, we make war!

The citizens all around start to reach within their pockets and shirts. They all hold up the same necklace with the chain, the bullet, and the key.

Citizen of Brassport: Those symbols have been the unity of our culture for many years. What you have just spoken to us is graven in our hearts. We fight for Abraham and New Brassport always. And if we fight for Abraham, that means we fight for you, too. The son is the father. The father is the son.

Steampunk looks around in amazement as he sees these people hold up what he thought was only his for the longest time. He looks over to see Cogsmire with his golden mask on, holding the same necklace out as well.

Cogsmire: I was honored to fight with your father and I'm just as honored to fight with you, Chase.

Steampunk feels an amazing joy as he witnesses this.

Hevy: Your father is part of the reason I am who I am today.

Hevy walks over to Steampunk and places his hand on his shoulder.

Hevy: He would be so proud to see you now.

Hevy has a smile on his face that is bigger than ever before.

Slinger: And you're like a brother to me. I couldn't be more thrilled to be by your side.

Jazz: I didn't know where I was going until I found this team. I'm with you until the end, bud.

Steampunk feels an intense determination upon hearing the allegiance of these great heroes.

He looks to see that Bucket is back and ready to fight. This catches him off guard.

Steampunk: Hudson... You're back!

Bucket: Yeah. They stitched me up. I wasn't supposed to leave the hospital yet, but I just couldn't help it. I had to see this through. So, I snuck out.

Slinger: Just in time too.

Bucket adjusts the bucket on his head so that he can see clearly out of the eye holes.

Bucket: That guy shot me in the leg, he's got to pay for that.

Bucket chuckles briefly.

Bucket: And besides, I still owe you for keying your car.

Steampunk walks over and shakes Hudson's hand.

Steampunk: Thank you for fighting with me, brother.

Gridd: You guys helped me locate my sister. I owe you everything for that. Soon, I will be reunited with her and the diamond will refuel Jettahawk once and for all.

Triggermate runs over to Steampunk.

Triggermate: I is happy to have being fighter with you Stimluck.

Steampunk shakes Triggermate's hand and grins at the mispronunciation of his name.

Steampunk: We must not forget those who have fallen today. This victory is for Drozer, Gold-bug, Clang, and Bolts, as well as the many lives lost at New Brassport to Ro*** Torch****.

The looks of determination turn into looks of sorrow as these recent deaths are remembered.

Steampunk: The same reason for fighting stands true for me today...

Chase remembers his anger towards Dawn earlier in his dream.

Steampunk: I fight in memory of Drake...

The Watcher nods at Steampunk

Steampunk: ...and win until Dawn returns.

The group pauses for a few minutes as they stare at the battle that awaits them.

Steampunk: Guns of Abraham. Tonight, we make war!

Each person lines up next to Steampunk as the army follows behind them. They slowly advance forward toward the stormy fortress.

Cogsmire holds his sword at his back. Gridd holds his Babylon Board next to him as his gravity bands begin to glow. Jazz holds his guitar by the neck, walking forward with his hat tipped down, covering his eyes. Bucket holds his gun at his shoulder, marching intently. Slinger arms his mechanical wings, ready to fly. The Watcher holds his gun blade ready to fire. Steampunk's shoulder gun moves from his back and into target mode. Hevy picks his "Barnstormer" off the ground and drags it behind him as they walk. Triggermate is no longer smiling as he usually would. Instead, he is filled with the will to fight as he detaches his sniper rifle, deploying it as two separate guns. The army of New Brassport marches as one united force, loaded and ready with their weapons and the power of their will.

The tower looms closer, lighting striking randomly inside it. Gridd looks closely at the ancient wreckage as they walk nearer to it.

Gridd: This capsule, where is it from?

Watcher: It's believed to be the wreckage of some ancient fleet.

Gridd: The markings on it. They're Babylonian. This is the wreckage from the ancient Jettahawk war.

Cogsmire: How would it end up on earth? Isn't Jettahawk in a different realm?

Gridd: It is. That's why none of this makes sense.

Hevy: Well whatever it is, you'll have the diamond back before the night ends. That is what's important.

Hevy hands Gridd the lightning whip that Bolts used before he died.

Hevy: I almost forgot, you're going to need more than just those fancy wristbands. Use this. Bolts wouldn't mind.

Gridd holds the deactivated whip in his hands and stares at it.

Gridd: I'm honored to use it. Thank you.

The team approaches at the entrance of the dome. They waste no time as they enter the arena.

In the middle of the arena stands Gladstone, in golden tinted metal armor. He holds a long bronze hammer in his right hand. In the middle of the arena is the Power Diamond. Its power is being drained as it runs through a tube and into Gladstone's armor.

Gladstone: The process is almost complete. All of it's power is about to be mine.

Gridd: That power has never been yours to use. And tonight, we're taking it back.

Gladstone breathes heavily as his armor and skin pulsates waves of red energy.

Gladstone: Good. I need someone to take this energy out on. And I see you brought some friends with you to help... Cute.

Cogsmire pumps his fist down causing his arm gun to shift forward then back into position. This action loads and readies the weapon.

Cogsmire: These are my people. The collective of New Brassport and the army of Abraham. You will terrorize us no longer.

Gladstone laughs.

Gladstone: That's great and all, but this fight doesn't involve them.

The Power Diamonds energy surges into Gladstone's right hand and he forces it forward into the crowd of fighters. A red wall forms and pushes the citizens outside of the dome. As they are forced out, the door closes, shutting them out.

Slinger: What are you doing? Why can't they fight with us?

Gladstone: Because the army you will be fighting is yourselves.

As Gladstone says this, nine red circles form on the ground.

Jazz: What is this?

The group backs up as red figures start to form from the circles.

Hevy studies the creatures carefully, noticing something unnerving.

Hevy: Wait a second, why is there a fat guy coming out of the ground?

Gridd: Hevy, I think that's you!

Gladstone: These nine clones are mirror images of yourselve.

Steampunk looks closely to see that the statement is true. Standing before them are nine, red, mirror-images of the Guns of Abraham.

Cogsmire: Are you really claiming that we will fight ourselves?

Gladstone: Each of these are just as strong and skilled as you've made them to be. There is no move you can make that they won't mimic. Have fun fighting your demons!

The mirror versions start to run forward.

Steampunk: Well here we go. War starts now.

The team runs forward to meet their attackers in a line formation. Cogsmire draws his sword and charges forward. The red Cogsmire does the same.

The two swords meet with a loud clash. After about five failed attempts to strike down his opponent, Cogsmire creates platforms in the air to jump around to the back. He swiftly evades a sword strike and hops on these platforms, striking downward on his enemy.

The red Cogsmire turns around and immediately blocks the attack.

Cogsmire takes a step back and the red Cogsmire does the same.

Cogsmire: You're a tough mate to beat! But alas...

Cogsmire holds his sword out in a pointing gesture.

Cogsmire: So am I!

He aims his wrist forward and rapidly fires from his wrist gun. The bullets spray out at a steady rate as blasts of magic launch from orbs above him.

The bullets break into the imposter magi as Cogsmire notices that the foe he is fighting is made of some kind of red glass. Each bullet causes shards of red glass to break off.

e: It appears I'm wearing him down more and _ by the minute!

Just as he says this, Gladstone shoots a beam of energy that regenerates the glossy exterior of the imposter.

Bucket shouts from the distance.

Bucket: We have to break them down faster than they can regenerate.

Watcher: We're going to need backup!

The Watcher dodges an attack from his imposter and drops a smoke pellet on the ground. In the shadow of this smoke, he sends a signal to some allies with the technology on his wrist.

Meanwhile, Cogsmire is still deep in combat.

He gets kicked down by his opponent as the foe fires his wrist gun. Cogsmire quickly creates a gear of magic to block the attack.

Cogsmire: I've had about enough of this tomfoolery!

Small gears are activated around the edge of his opponent's sword. These gears spin rapidly, making the sword into a grinding weapon. He slams the sword down on Cogsmire's shield. Sparks fly off of the shield as he struggles to keep it up.

Cogsmire: What a minute? If your sword can do that...

Cogsmire looks down at his sword and presses a button on the handle. This action causes the same gears to activate on his sword.

Cogsmire: So can mine!

Cogsmire quickly sweeps the leg of his imposter, causing him to fall. He then swings his upgraded sword down on the fallen enemy causing shards of glass to fly off in bigger chunks.

Nearby, Slinger and his double are engaged in combat above. He takes a long swoop around the arena as he gauges what his opponent will do next. They both circle the air like vultures. He waits for the best opening, then quickly swoops in to attack.

As he dives faster and faster, he tries to target his enemy with the tech in his goggles. He finally locks onto his target.

Slinger: Stay put!

He fires both his rotating handguns but the red Slinger quickly dodges them, swooping up to tackle Slinger in the air. The two speed towards the ground. When they make contact, Slinger's wings crack and break off as they smash into the ground.

Slinger: No... Not my wings!

He forcefully kicks the imposter off of him and the two engage in hand to hand combat.

Much to Slinger's dismay, each punch is dodged and evaded. The silent foe finally punches him directly in the chest. This breaks Slinger's chest plate into pieces, and he lays on the ground nearly unconscious.

Bucket notices this and turns to shoot at Slinger's opponent. The surprise attack works and knocks the enemy down.

Gladstone: Look at you! Fools! You can't even beat yourselves. Why on earth would you be deserving of the diamond?

Bucket turns to engage in combat with his doppelgänger. He jumps and quickly kicks the foe down, only for red Bucket to immediately spring back up and kick him with equal force.

Bucket: Someone go after Gladstone!

Gridd: We can't! These things are too powerful!

Bucket fires, but this attack is avoided as well.

The enemy jumps forward and punches bucket in the head. This causes his bucket to fall off and land on the ground. He immediately grabs the titanium headgear and swings it forward with menacing force. It smashes his ruby-colored foe in the head and his bucket falls off as well. This causes the imposter to pick up his bucket and swing it at Bucket's head. The attack/counter battle continues for quite some time.

Jazz has his guitar in axe mode, as does his red opponent. They both swing their axes at each other, and each attack is met with a loud clang of weaponry.

Jazz rolls on the ground to avoid the down swinging motion of the red Jazz's axe. Once this attack misses, he springs up to knock his opponent down. The red Jazz lays on the ground, while Jazz places his foot on his chest. He holds his clawed right hand up.

Jazz: This is going to hurt you more than it hurts me... I think.

He swiftly slashes his hand across his opponent's face and shards of red glass break off, leaving a gaping hole in the side of his head. Jazz holds his axe high in the air and prepares to swing it down.

Suddenly, a blast of red energy soars out from his attacker's hands. This sends Jazz in the air, only for him to hit the ground hard. Jazz quickly gets up and switches his guitar to gun mode. He strums chords as fast as he can, to fire as many rounds as possible, but no damage is done.

Jazz: They're too powerful. We can't beat them!

Steampunk sees the red Jazz approaching the fallen Jazz. He quickly takes action, and fires his shoulder gun at the enemy.

This attack doesn't last long as Steampunk's mirror image is preparing to attack him.

They both run at each other and activate their chainsaw attachments. Both chainsaws make contact, and intense sparks fly from the heated epicenter of the twisted metal.

Steampunk looks deeply into the eyes of his red self, as it appears to be overpowering him.

Cogsmire takes a break from fighting his opponent to use his magic to push the evil Steampunk back.

With this brief opening, Steampunk rains down gunfire onto his enemy's chest.

Steampunk: This ends now!

The firepower blows a hole through the attacker's chest and he falls to the ground. Chase turns around to quickly try and attack Gladstone while he has the chance.

He fires a missile out of his back and it launches toward the powered Gladstone. Just as the missile is about to make contact, Gladstone fires a blast of red energy that makes the missile explode in the air.

Gladstone: It's going to take much more than a well-placed missile to destroy me boy!

Steampunk feels rage build up inside him, but is quickly interrupted by a strike to the back. He turns around to see that his opponent has regenerated once again.

Steampunk: You've got to be kidding me.

Gridd has at this point activated Bolt's lightning whips.

He swings them forward and they wrap around his foe. He struggles to break free as Gridd focuses the electricity around him. Gridd quickly activates his Babylon Board and hovers ahead, dragging the imposter behind him.

The enemy fires gravity shots at Gridd, but he maneuvers to dodge the attacks.

As he cuts through the air, the red Gridd finally makes contact with one of his attacks. The gravity blast hits Gridd hard and the shift of momentum knocks him off his board.

Gridd quickly recovers and runs to attack. The mirror Gridd locks him in a gravity hold and the real Gridd quickly does the same. Both gravity charges are held together in one spot and the energy builds. The atmosphere around the orb sends heavy soundwaves out across the dome. The colors within the charge shift into the negative spectrum.

Gridd: Everyone get down! This is going to be bad!

Everyone in the dome starts to float above the ground slowly. The gravity shift is intense and impossible to fight.

Finally, the blast erupts and launches throughout the arena. All of the mirrored imposters dissipate in the blast.

Everyone is sent flying in different directions. Steampunk hits the ground next to Hevy. Bucket, Jazz, and Slinger land in a group. Triggermate, Jazz, Cogsmire and the Watcher are scattered elsewhere.

Gladstone steps closer to Steampunk. His armor still shines a bright red.

Gladstone: Things are different now. You can't overpower me as easily as you could The Royale.

Steampunk tries to lift himself up.

Steampunk: You can't win Gladstone. I can't let you! This will end.

Gladstone swings his hammer and its weight crushes into Steampunk's chest. A loud, thunderous boom echoes out. His armor cracks and shatters as he is sent flying across the ground once more.

The Power Diamond fires out hundreds of beams into the field. Each beam creates a red flame that slowly crystalizes into an armored fighter.

Steampunk lays on the ground with his armor damaged. He struggles to stay conscious with the force of the attack nearly knocking him out.

Hevy: Get up kid, we have to finish this!

Cogsmire grabs Steampunk and tries to lift him.

The army of red, glasslike soldiers continues to fill the field.

The rest of the team regroups and stands in a line side by side as Gladstone walks toward them.

As Gladstone walks, his army follows closely behind him, in perfect, synchronized steps.

Triggermate runs in front of Steampunk as the others try and help him up. He takes aim at Gladstone.

Triggermate: No more hurt my friend!

Gladstone holds his hand out, and red energy immediately surrounds Triggermate.

Gladstone: Get out of my way, lizard freak!

Gladstone moves his hand outward and Triggermate is swiftly tossed to the side. The others try to attack, but he quickly locks them into a frozen position with the energy of the Power Diamond.

Gridd: What is this! This is not how the diamond is supposed to be used. You need to stop this now!

Cogsmire tries to overpower the red energy with his magic.

Cogsmire: Get up! He's going to kill you!

Slinger: Come on Chase! I can't lose you!

Chase tries his best to lift himself up. He looks around the see that everything is blurry. All he can hear is the muffled screams of his teammates yelling at him to get up and fight. This seems to be the end for him.

Gladstone approaches Chase and kicks him. This knocks Chase down once more.

Gladstone: Look at yourself. It's pathetic.

Steampunk: I... I...

Gladstone bends down to look at him.

Gladstone: What? Just say it.

Steampunk: I... Give up.

These words strike the others harder than any weapon, as they are held into place by Gladstone.

Gladstone: Heh. Yeah... You do, don't you.

Gladstone slowly lifts his hammer up.

Gladstone: I'm sorry kid, but I have a cause to fight for too.

Steampunk looks up to see his fate approaching. He closes his eyes, ready to accept his death. Time seems to slow down as he thinks his last thoughts.

Steampunk: This must have been what it felt like when the Master Royale looked up to see his fate on Judgement Day. This diamond's power. It's too great. Now that it has been used against me, I see now that no one should use its energy to fight. Not even me. The commander was right, I'm no better than Gladstone. I'm no better than The Royale. I have to be stopped.

Steampunk pauses for a moment before thinking the next thought.

Steampunk: I'm sorry dad. This isn't the type of war I want to make.

He breathes out heavily as he awaits the crushing blow of the warhammer.

A few seconds go by and nothing happens. He feels the rumbling of the entry door opening once more. Steampunk opens his eyes to see that Gladstone has dropped his hammer.

Gladstone: What is this?

The citizens of New Brassport step away from the now-opened entrance. They look in the distance to see someone is approaching at high speed.

Gladstone: No... It can't be!

Watcher: Our reinforcements have arrived.

The supernatural lock is released and the Guns of Abraham reorganize into a fighting stance.

Steampunk lifts his head to see Gladstone fearfully stepping back. Suddenly, short blasts of blue break into surrounding enemies with precise hits.

Gladstone: It's not slowing down!

Steampunk begins to put things together, realizing where these attacks are coming from. Suddenly, Gladstone is launched across the dome as a blue streak zooms by.

Steampunk whispers under his breath.

Steampunk: Flashpoint.

Cogsmire and Slinger help lift Steampunk to his feet as Flashpoint moves throughout the horde of enemies.

Cogsmire: Jolly good show! Who is this rather speedy lad?

Steampunk is finally raised to a standing position as he picks up his gun.

Steampunk: He's my friend, and he's just saved us.

Suddenly, a flash of red enters the arena.

The trail of blue and red cease and the two speedsters are finally revealed. Flashpoint reaches out to shake Steampunk's hand.

Flashpoint: It's been, awhile. Hasn't it.

Steampunk: You could say that.

Flashpoint and Steampunk have not seen each other since they both left The Redeemers. Not much has changed. Flashpoint still wears his black and blue armored suit. The Speed Diamond shines bright as it is held in the chest of his suit.

Hevy: That's a pretty nifty bow you got their kid.

Flashpoint holds his bow next to his side. It shines its usual blue.

He looks back at Steampunk.

Flashpoint: Looks like you've made a few friends since we last met. I want you to meet my half-brother. This is Isaac Korver.

Watcher: We call him Crossfire.

Crossfire stands next to Flashpoint. His suit is very similar to his brother's. The only difference is that it is red. In his chest is a red diamond that looks very similar to the Power Diamond. In both of his hands, he holds crossbows with short, bright red arrows locked into place.

Crossfire: Nice to meet you.

Crossfire turns to The Watcher.

Crossfire: You better be glad I saw your call when I did. Me and Noah were just about to close up things over at the mansion.

Gladstone's army crowds around him as he tries to stand. They look at him aimlessly, not knowing what to do after this sudden surprise attack.

Steampunk: How can you run fast like him? Isn't there only one Speed Diamond?

Crossfire: This one is synthetic. It's not the same as what he has. It's…

Jazz: Guys, can we talk about this later? He's getting back up.

Flashpoint: Is that a guitar? Why do you have a guitar on the battlefield?

Jazz doesn't answer, turning instead to see the armored citizens of New Brassport entering the dome to fight.

The people run quickly to meet their friends. Their numbers have now significantly increased.

Brassport Soldier: The door was quite the task. Luckily, we were able to open it.

Gladstone stands and sees the new army formed.

Flashpoint, Steampunk, Bucket, Slinger, Hevy, Cogsmire, Triggermate, Crossfire, The Watcher, Gridd and Jazz all group together and stand in a line. The Brassport army stands behind them with their weapons ready.

Gladstone: Fine! Bring your army!

Gladstone slams his bronze hammer on the ground as a large number of red soldiers form from the diamond.

Gladstone: But I'll bring mine!

Flashpoint draws his bow, Steampunk's shoulder gun starts to spin, Bucket places his gun on his shoulder, Slinger readies his guns, Hevy's "Barnstormer" spins and heats up.

Cogsmire holds his sword in front of him as the gears inside it begin to spin. In his other hand, he creates a gear of magic energy around his arm. Triggermate strikes his tail on the ground while aiming his sniper rifle. Crossfire connects both of his crossbows together and they snap into place, creating one big dual-firing bow.

The Watcher holds his gun blade nearby, ready to attack. Jazz holds his guitar in firing mode, and Gridd activates his Babylon board once more, while also activating his lightning whips.

The citizens of New Brassport roar their battle cries behind the line of heroes.

Cogsmire: Our army is smaller but we fight as one, unified force. Your hivemind of reckless destruction cannot overpower what we have.

Gladstone: And what's that?

The two sides prepare for attack as battle cries from both sound out.

Cogsmire: Heritage.

Both sides erupt into chaos. Steampunk and Bucket stay in place and fire their weapons while others charge forward into direct, melee attacks. The two sides clash in the middle and shards of red glass fly in all directions.

Gladstone stands in place and uses the diamond's power to regenerate the fallen fighters.

Crossfire and Flashpoint speed through the forces in a crisscross pattern, shooting many of them down with their red and blue energy arrows as they zoom by.

Flashpoint: Isaac! Scale the wall. We'll take them from above.

The two run at insane speeds toward the curved wall of the arena. They both run along the wall as they spiral up.

Slinger looks up to see Flashpoint's blue speed trail moving quickly around the wall as well as Crossfire's red speed trail moving counterclockwise along the wall. Out of Crossfire's bow fires two rapid streams of arrows, while Flashpoint's only reigns down one arrow every two seconds.

The arrows pierce down through the unsuspecting army as the two continue to speed along the wall.

Slinger: Chase! You used to fight with that guy?

Steampunk activates his chainsaw attachment and forces it into an approaching enemy.

Steampunk: Sure did.

A fighter jumps onto Slinger's back and he quickly spins to throw him off.

Slinger: Why'd you ever leave that team? This is awesome!

Slinger picks up speed and jumps to plant both feet on an attacker's chest. He forcefully kicks him down while firing his guns rapidly.

The Watcher fights nearby with Jazz by his side. Jazz switches between firing his guitar and swinging his axe at the circle of enemies around him. The Watcher swings his gun blade in big, sweeping slashes, and periodically fires rounds from the blade as he swings.

Jazz: I've got to say, I never thought I'd be fighting with a guy like you.

The Watcher flips over an oncoming foe as Jazz shoots the enemy down.

Watcher: Touché.

Jazz ducks to avoid an attack. He quickly punches the enemy onto the ground. The Watcher grabs a handgun strapped to his ankle and fires it three times into the fallen enemy. Five more soldiers attack the Watcher from behind.

Three Brassport fighters run to his aid.

Brassport Soldier: Get away, knave!

The female soldier grabs the crystalline humanoid from the Watcher's back and throws him off.

The three Brassportians proceed to fire their guns, taking out ten of the surrounding enemies.

Triggermate runs around frantically firing at the soldiers around him. Five Brassport fighters flank him, firing as well.

Hevy stands nearby and unleashes the "Barnstormer." The three streams of bullets pour out like beams of fire as his miniguns spin rapidly. Large numbers of attackers break and fall, only to regenerate shortly after.

Hevy: They're not staying down! Nothing has changed. They're still getting right back up!

Gridd flies by on his board as Flashpoint runs off of the wall. Flashpoint slows down as his Speed Diamond recharges. He runs at the same speed of Gridd's board.

Flashpoint: You have any projectile attacks?

Gridd fires off two gravity shots from his hands.

Flashpoint: I'll take that as a "yes."

Flashpoint unhooks his bow into two melee weapons.

Flashpoint: Keep firing! I'll help you out.

Flashpoint speeds forward and rapidly attacks the soldiers with his two weapons as Brassport fighters attack from the distance. Gridd soars near the ground and fires gravity shots from one hand while whipping through other enemies with the lightning whip in the other hand.

Flashpoint runs out of view as the bands on Gridd's arms begin to glow. He makes a sharp turn, and the gravity around him starts to shift and focus. Enemies all around fly into the air slightly as he swings his momentum around and sharply turns. The gravity releases and the enemies are sent flying forward with Gridd.

Gridd: Cog! I'm bringing them to you!

Gridd soars forward carrying a collection of enemies in a wake behind him. He activates both lighting whips and holds them at his sides. The whips wrap around foes as he speeds by.

Cogsmire opens myriad portals and Gridd abruptly stops, sending the enemies behind him into the portals, as well as the ones being dragged by his whips.

Cogsmire: Good shot mate!

Cogsmire turns to fire his arm gun into five enemies. He holds three more in place with yellow, magic gears. While they are held there, he swings his sword into enemies one by one. He holds the grinding gears of the sword into each before moving to the next. Triggermate and Crossfire approach him and attack as well.

Crossfire detaches his two crossbows and begins to fire both of them. The red energy arrows fire much faster than those from a regular bow.

Cogsmire fires a blast of magic from one hand while shooting his arm gun on the other. Crossfire stands to the right of him while firing and Triggermate fires as well from his left.

Triggermate: Teamwork yay!

On the other side of the dome, Steampunk and Slinger are engaged in heavy combat.

Slinger: We need backup over here!

Steampunk forcefully swings the chainsaw of his massive gun down on the horde of enemies that have tackled him, while his shoulder gun autotargets other enemies and fires.

Suddenly, a missile is fired from afar by a Brassportian fighter, and the enemies are scattered away in a destructive explosion.

Slinger: Help me!

Steampunk: Dude…

Slinger: SOMEONE GET THEM OFF ME!

Steampunk: Slinger, look!

Slinger opens his eyes to see that the enemies around them have been destroyed by a teenage Brassport girl in the distance. Smoke pours out from the barrel of her rocket launcher and she smiles at Slinger.

Slinger: Oh... Wow. She's beautiful.

Slinger starts to wave back but is quickly knocked over by a falling enemy.

The girl runs over and shoots the enemy off of Slinger. She grabs his hand and helps him up.

Slinger: Thanks... What's your name.

The girl look up at him with hazel eyes. She wears a helmet but has strands of bright red hair hanging out in the front.

???: My name is Amber Rose. My friends call me Firefly.

Slinger: Are we friends then?

Firefly: Ha ha! Yeah, we are.

Steampunk: That's great and all, but can we finish this?

Firefly reaches into a bag connected to her belt and pulls out two boomerangs. She holds them in an "x" pattern and throws them forward. They ricochet off of many enemies and eventually, a pellet inside is launched out of them and explodes before the boomerangs come back to her.

Not too far away, Bucket has fallen to the ground and many enemies have piled on top of him.

Bucket: Help me! I'm going down.

Triggermate notices, and hurriedly runs to his aid. His tail wags behind him and strikes enemies.

Triggermate jumps in the air, firing down on the enemies tackling Bucket. While in the air - much to his surprise - the enemies scatter away and Bucket is left open.

Triggermate is falling fast and tries to find a safe place to land.

Bucket: Don't worry bud! I've got you!

Triggermate places his gun on his back and opens his arms, preparing himself for Bucket's rescue.

Suddenly, in the distance, Gladstone yells.

Gladstone: Masquerade, now!

Bucket quickly pulls out a long dagger.

Cogsmire turns to see this, and grabs one of Abraham's stopwatches from his pocket.

He presses the button on top, and all time miraculously slows down.

Everything around Cogsmire goes quiet as time slows to a snail's pace. He runs forward as fast as he can. All he can hear is the ticking of the stopwatch in his pocket.

Cogsmire: NO! Get off of him!

He tries his best to reach Triggermate before the dagger stabs him. In front of him is the horrifying scene of his friend slowly falling into the hidden dagger in Bucket's hand.

He quickly fires a magic spell, but it moves nowhere as everything is effected by the slowing of time. Cogsmire is the only object in the whole scene that can move at normal speed.

Cogsmire: No... Don't fall on it! Please!

Cogsmire begins to cry, realizing that he won't be fast enough to save Triggermate from the blade. He looks ahead to see the sharp point piercing into his abdomen. A screech of pain forms on his lips, as the weight of his fall forces the blade deeper. The stopwatch's effects begin to wear off and time moves back to normal.

Cogsmire: GET OFF HIM!

Cogsmire forcefully tackles Bucket as Triggermate falls off of the dagger.

Cogsmire: Who are you!

He rips the bucket off of his head and throws it to the side. To his horror, underneath is no longer Hudson's face but the blank face of Masquerade.

Cogsmire: How did you escape? Answer me now!

Cogsmire's tears pour out of the eye holes of his bronze mask.

Hevy runs to the scene and throws his "Barnstormer" to the side. He then grabs Masquerade by the neck and holds him in the air.

Hevy: I've been through too much today! You've angered the wrong man! Where's the real Bucket! Start talking... now!

Masquerade: There are many of my kind, Mr. Hevy. I could be anyone. Your next-door neighbor, your governor, the head of Surge Tower. I am but a small piece of the Masquerade. We are many, we are legion, we are...

Hevy: Don't care!

Hevy immediately slams Masquerade's head into the ground multiple times.

Hevy: Where. Is. BUCKET!

Masquerade struggles to speak as blood trickles down his blank face.

Masquerade: Well, where did you leave him last?

Hevy: I swear, if you did anything to that kid…

Hevy pauses.

Masquerade: You'll do what?

Hevy: This…

Hevy grabs Masquerade and spins him around before throwing him high into the air. He then quickly grabs his "Barnstormer" and completely unleashes havoc from the gun into the man as he flies into the air. The bullets completely destroy Masquerade, as his limbs and huge parts of his body break off into bullet-riddled pieces.

His body falls to the ground in four segments, and Hevy pants angrily as rage fills his body.

Cogsmire: Triggermate… Look at me!

Cogsmire removes the mask from his face and bends down to look at the deep wound in Triggermate's abdomen.

Triggermate: Cogsmortemer… I… I has… last… thing to say.

Cogsmire cries heavier, realizing there is nothing he can do to save his friend.

Cogsmire: I'm listening mate. I'm all ears.

Triggermate places his scaly hand on Cogsmire's face. His hand shakes as he struggles to lift it up.

Triggermate: I is happy... to has been... friendship... with you.

He grins his usual grin one last time.

Triggermate: Triggermate will... always... fight... for you.

Cogsmire places his friend's head on the ground gently. He looks one last time at Triggermate as he passes.

Cogsmire: Always mate... Always.

He presses the button on his stopwatch one more time to stretch out this final moment with Triggermate. Everything around him slows. The enemies around him cease to move.

All is frozen to a halt.

Cogsmire slowly stands.

Everything is silent.

He looks at his fallen friend for as long as he can.

He clears his throat and finally speaks to himself, his words echoing through the arena locked in time-stasis.

Cogsmire: This must end now.

Slowly, the arena unfreezes and time starts again.

Cogsmire stands as two Brassport fighters gently pick up Triggermate's body and carry him out of the arena.

Tears pour down his face as he watches his reptilian friend exit from his view.

Cogsmire looks completely enraged as he reaches down to grab his mask. He places it on his face

He turns to face the entire approaching army.

Hevy: Buddy, we... we have to finish this. I'm sorry.

Cogsmire lets out a single sigh.

Cogsmire: And finish it... I shall.

He places his hands together as yellow energy forms in a collected space between his hands. The energy grows and grows. Cogsmire begins to shout.

The enemies slowly back up as the energy grows even stronger. Cogsmire at this point is screaming with rage.

The energy has grown to almost twice Cogsmire's size.

Cogsmire: I've lost too much today. You've taken my city, my brothers, and worst of all... You've taken my Triggermate!

Suddenly, from the ball of energy, multiple chains of light fly into the chests of each enemy. One by one, the foes are pierced and enraptured by the energy chains.

Steampunk looks out to see streams of light chains launching in clusters from Cogsmire to fill the field, as each and every enemy is captured by them.

Cogsmire: You will not take this victory from me.

Energy forms at the base of his feet as he prepares to launch himself into the air, carrying the entire opposing army with him.

Gridd: Finish this!

Cogsmire lets an echoing roar sound out as he forcefully rockets himself into the air. Soaring higher and higher, the glasslike enemies are dragged behind him. They clash and break together as the chains pool into one spot behind him. Each of them are dragged heavenward.

The rest of the team looks in wonder at this amazing spectacle.

Flashpoint: We need him on the team.

Watcher: Yeah, we really do.

Cogsmire finally reaches the pinnacle of his jump high above the opening of the arena.

He uses all his might to turn backwards as now faces the arena ground.

The hundreds of foes slowly turn in a roundabout circle high in the air. Cogsmire uses the little energy he has left to swing the enemies hurdling back at the arena.

One by one they are detached from the chain and sent flying towards the ground.

Slinger: Get out of the way! They're coming in fast!

Flashpoint cuts through and moves each team member out of the way in the blink of an eye, as the red soldiers smash and break into the ground.

The hordes of them cover the ground in shards as they break beyond any point of regeneration.

Gladstone: Unbelievable.

The final few enemies fall to their fate.

Jazz: On no!

Brassport Citizen: Our leader! He's falling.

Crossfire speeds towards the center of the arena in an attempt to catch Cogsmire as he falls.

Crossfire: He's coming in too fast!

Crossfire speeds towards Hevy and grabs him.

Crossfire: Here, you do it.

Hevy: Um… Okay?

Hevy shifts around trying to position himself in the right place to catch him.

Cogsmire speeds downward faster and faster, like a meteor to the ground.

Slinger: Don't mess this up!

As Cogsmire finally comes within a few feet of Hevy, he jumps to catch him. Cogsmire slams into Hevy and they both smash into the ground.

Hevy lets out a shout of pain as he breaks Cogsmire's fall.

Watcher: Hevy! Are you okay? Speak to me.

Hevy, knocked completely unconscious, does not respond.

Brassport Citizen: Cogsmire! Are you alive? He's not responding!

Steampunk and the rest of the team run to the scene.

Jazz: He completely drained his power.

Steampunk: He completely cleared the field as well.

In the distance, Gladstone looks around to see the carnage of his soldiers scattered across the field in shards of red.

Gladstone: That's enough! I will not let this continue!

Gladstone conjures up all the energy he can from the Power Diamond and extends his hand out to fire it.

Brassport Commander: Citizens! Unleash!

The soldiers of Brassport all line up and create a barricade around the Guns of Abraham.

Firefly: We will protect our leader at all costs!

Each soldier aims their weapon at Gladstone and await the command.

Commander: FIRE!

The line of soldiers fires their weapons and a sea of firepower soars toward Gladstone. The bullets bounce off his armor and he is unaffected by the intense firepower.

Gridd: It's no use!

Gladstone: This is my last resort! Your bullets will never break me!

Brassport Commander: AND YOU WILL NOT BREAK US!

Gladstone smiles as he unleashes this intense attack. Red energy fills the arena as the soldiers fly in all directions.

Steampunk: No!

The other team members grab Hevy and Cogsmire's unconscious bodies and desperately try to drag them away from the attack. Eventually the attack hits them and the team is launched away.

Gladstone advances toward the fallen team with energy radiating throughout him.

Gladstone: This is how it will always end! If you take down The Royale, someone else steps in. You may win the battles...

Gladstone armor starts to grow and grow as more layers form around him. His stature stretches higher and he towers over everyone.

Gladstone: ...but I will win the war!

Steampunk and Jazz exchange a look of horror as Gladstone grows into his final form.

Steampunk: Get up!

Jazz: Chase... Look at this! We can't win this.

Nearby, Flashpoint stands to help The Watcher up as well.

Watcher: Maybe not, but we will always keep fighting.

Gladstone's armor reaches its final titan like form and he stands in the middle of the coliseum. He looks around at the fallen heroes.

Gladstone: This is the end of the line for Brassport!

He reaches down and picks up Steampunk in his colossal hand.

Gladstone: And this is the end for you too.

Steampunk tries with all he can to move and free himself, but the blast of the last attack renders him helpless.

Crossfire and Flashpoint fire all they can at Gladstone but these attacks prove futile.

Watcher: This can't be the end. We can't lose another Redeemer.

Flashpoint: We have to do something!

Just as Flashpoint says this, Gladstone throws Steampunk into the ground with a cratering blow.

He then quickly turns to kick the watcher down and into the ground.

Jazz and Gridd try to run, but Gladstone reaches them before they can escape. He grabs Gridd's Babylon Board and throws it across the field before punching them across the ground with devastating force.

Slinger is grabbed by his feet and thrown to the side, smashing into the wall.

Gladstone: This is what it's like to have full unbridled power! A feeling you know too well. But now, it's mine… And you must pay for trying to stop this.

The Brassport soldiers scatter, trying to escape the full-force attacks of the titanic Gladstone.

Gladstone's hammer soars into his hand and grows to match the size of his grown armor. He swings the hammer high above his head, preparing to finish his task.

Gladstone: This is it! Steampunk, look at me.

Steampunk looks up at Gladstone through his broken mask.

Gladstone: I. WIN.

Suddenly, red and blue flames form all around the arena. In the blink of an eye, a large strike of white slashes across Gladstone and he falls to the ground with an earth-shattering thud.

Out of the flames emerges a tall black figure. Thick smoke billows out of the ground, mixed with red and blue flames.

Watcher: What is that?

The team looks on in amazement as one red and one blue eye shine through the smoke as The Lost Titan comes into view.

The Lost Titan lets out a hellish roar.

Lost Titan: By the power of Akarius and the Dark Dwelling, you will not prevail!

The team is completely speechless until Jazz finally says:

Jazz: There is an actual Dinosaur-man creature thing on the field. This is actually happening.

The Lost Titan towers much higher above Gladstone and begins to punch away huge pieces of armor from him.

Gladstone: What is this? Who are you?

The Lost Titan picks up Gladstone and rapidly slams him on the ground over and over again.

Gladstone picks up his hammer and swings it up at the Titan in a desperate attempt to fight back. The Lost Titan grabs the hammer and crushes it in his hand.

Gladstone: IMPOSSIBLE!

The team looks in amazement as this unknown ally saves them.

Gideon jumps out of Maug and goes soaring through the air. Blue and red flames billow from each hand. He hits the ground and rolls...

Gladstone: GET AWAY FROM....

His sentence is cut short as Gideon punches straight through his chest. A hole in his chest plate is burned around the entry of the wound. Everyone watches in complete shock as blood pours out of his chest.

Gideon: You are finished!

His eyes burn blue and red as he says this, and Gladstone slowly turns to dust, falling to the dirt. All that is left is a charred skeleton as he hits the ground.

Steampunk looks to see the eyes of his long-lost cousin.

Steampunk: Gideon?

Gideon: Come find me.

Gideon and Maug immediately disappear leaving nothing but scorched earth beneath them.

Gladstone had been defeated.

The day was won.

Crossfire: Well... That just happened.

Gridd runs over to grab his Babylon Board.

Watcher: Who was that?

Steampunk is still in shock.

Slinger: Chase, that really was him. Wasn't it?

Steampunk: Yeah, it was... But how?

Gridd grabs the Power Diamond.

At this point, Hevy starts to wake up.

Hevy: What... What happened?

He says this as he looks to see the wreckage on the field.

Jazz approaches Hevy and the still-unconscious Cogsmire.

Jazz: A *lot* happened.

Hevy: Did we win?

Jazz looks around one last time.

Jazz: Yeah... We did.

They both smile and let out a sigh.

Gridd walks over to the Watcher, holding the diamond.

Gridd: It's time to take this home.

The Watcher places his hand on Gridd's shoulder.

Watcher: It's time to find your sister as well.

Steampunk and the rest of the fighters all collect in the middle of the arena.

Steampunk: I'm going to go find out where Bucket is.

Brassport fighter: We're coming with you. We need to get Cogsmire some help.

Steampunk nods as three citizens pick up Cogsmire.

He looks down at the key around his chest.

Steampunk: Dad. We did it.

The Truth of Judgement Day

The Watcher enters one of the storage rooms within the Redeemer's mansion. In the middle of the dark room is a round table. He removes his mask and places it on the table, revealing his face.

Drake rubs his eyes after the long day he had and turns to the touchscreen behind him. On the screen, he writes the names Gridd and Cogsmire next to his own name. In the middle, he writes:

How are we clones?

We look identical to each other but none of us know why?

Further research is necessary.

He taps the screen and the file closes. Next to this newly created file is another file titled, "Bedrock Arc Research".

???: Drake Barrows?

Drake turns around rapidly as this unknown voice calls out from the shadows.

Drake immediately draws his gun blade, ready to attack.

Drake: Step Forward! Who are you?

The mysterious figure steps out of the shadows, revealing himself to be none other than the Watcher of Brassport.

Drake places the gun blade back in its sheath.

Drake: What are you doing here? How did you get in here? Two Watchers aren't supposed to be seen in the same place, you know that!

Watcher B: How did you escape Judgement Day?

Drake looks confused.

Drake: Why should I tell you?

Watcher B: Because you agreed to be a Watcher, and that means honesty... always. That's why I'm here, to be open with you about something you don't know. But first, you must be open with me. What happened that day?

Drake breathes in deeply and recounts what happened that day.

Drake: The Watcher before me, he was a friend of mine, you could say. He helped me prepare and form this team. He was Watcher Number 1, to be exact.

Watcher B: Can you be more specific?

Drake: His name was Ryan Martel. He was a brave man. He died in my place.

Drake pauses for a moment after saying this.

Drake: Right before judgment day started. We switched. We switched armor, names... I even gave him my powers. He became The Redeemer, and I vowed right then and there to become The Watcher in his place.

The Watcher of Brassport speaks up after this.

Watcher B: So he died when that bomb dropped... Not you? Why?

Drake: It was his idea. I was more than ready to give my life to defeat The Royale. We always knew that someone would have to stay when the bomb dropped. But he insisted that he be the one to do it. That man, Martel... He lost everything. He lost his family, his closest friend. I guess he thought the last thing he had to live for was seeing the Royale perish.

Watcher B: I don't mean to backtrack on you, but when you say you gave him your powers... Do you mean... These powers?

The Watcher of Brassport ignites his hand into flames right before Drake's eyes. Drake takes a few steps back as he realizes what this means.

Drake: You... You don't mean? You're... You...

Watcher B: Martel didn't die that day, Drake.

The Watcher of Brassport slowly removes his brass colored, battle-withered skull mask and lays it on the table.

Drake: Ryan... You're alive!

Before his eyes stands the man who started the path of Redemption years ago. Ryan Martel stands before him, alive and well.

Martel: Yes... I am. And I know you probably have several questions, and I will explain.

Drake interrupts him.

Drake: How could this happen! I became the Watcher in your place... But you were alive the whole time? Orion City has, for the past six months, been mourning the loss of The Redeemer and I've had to sit idly by and say nothing as they wondered who would protect them! I need answers, Ryan!

Ryan looks Drake in the eyes as he sees the confusion and shock on his face. An eerie tension hangs in the room.

Drake: If I didn't die that day... And you didn't... Who did? Don't tell me... Oh, God... Is Michael still out there?

Martel: Breathe Drake... Let me explain... Sit down.

Drake regains his composure and tries his best to regulate his panic long enough to hear what Ryan has to say.

Martel: The bomb was seconds from dropping as I held Michael there. You and the rest of the team had been warped away. This is what happened after that. This is the truth of Judgment Day.

(Six months ago)

Judgment Day

Ryan Martel is fully armored as The Redeemer as he holds Drake's brother Michael, who at the time was the Master Royale, steady as they both prepare to accept their fate.

Michael: Let me see your face brother. Let me see it one last time, please.

The Redeemer hesitates to do this but eventually takes off the mask.

Michael: I'm confused, you look very different than I remember.

Redeemer: People change Michael. You're living proof of that.

Michael struggles to keep the bomb in the air. He winces in pain.

Michael: Please forgive me! I lost my way.

I went down this horrible path and I've hurt so many people.

I didn't ever mean for it to come to this.

Redeemer: People never do.

But you were destroying so many things.

Things that didn't deserve it.

This had to happen Michael… I'm sorry.

Tears fall down Michael's face as he focuses what little energy he has left on holding the bomb in the air.

Redeemer: Your life here on earth was filled with evil.

You hurt so many people for your own pleasure.

The Redeemer takes the Power Diamond out of his chest. His suit stops glowing red. He throws the diamond to the side. The diamond rolls into the portal. The portal closes shortly after.

Redeemer: Your destructive nature has cost many lives.

Tears start to stream down his face.

Redeemer: But I do forgive you.

Not because you deserve it, but because redemption is for everyone, no matter how evil they are.

Michael begins to sob deeply as the reality of this hits him. He for once realizes the pain he has caused. It is too late for him to go back and fix it now.

Michael: Thank you, brother.

The two look up one last time at the bomb.

Redeemer: I'll accept this fate with you and we will both enter eternity with a clean slate.

Michael holds the bomb for one final minute.

He looks at The Redeemer and nods his head.

The bomb begins to fall.

Redeemer: Take my hand brother.

Redemption awaits us.

The top of the arena closes and the cylinder is sealed, containing the blast within.

Michael takes his brother's hand as the bomb falls faster and faster towards them.

The nuclear bomb is seconds away from exploding.

Suddenly, The Redeemer reaches within his cloak and holds in his hand a stopwatch. He, without hesitation, presses the nob at the top of the watch.

All time slows down around him the second he presses this; and the bomb seems to almost halt in the sky.

He looks down at the stop watch and opens it up to see the engravement, "a gift to Ryan from Abraham." This watch had been given to Ryan a few years back, before he ever became The Watcher. Abraham had told him that if he ever found himself in a situation that he couldn't escape, to press the watch and he would escape.

These words came to his mind after he had only moments ago said to Michael that his fate could not be escaped.

He looks up at the sky to see the bomb, as well as everything else, halted to a stop. He looks at the tears falling from Michael face.

The Redeemer says to himself.

Redeemer: You have the face of repentance… Maybe… You can have another chance at life.

He thinks to himself about how this goes against everything he and Drake had planned, but decides to save Michael, and give him a second chance.

He sits there in the silence and the peace of the frozen time around him.

Redeemer: Cogsmire! It's time!

These words echo through the silent coliseum.

Redeemer: Take us to the real Brassport.

A portal opens up below the two and they fall in as time resumes. They fall into the industrial steam-powered New Brassport City dimension, and the portal above them closes.

Michael breaks away from the frozen time lapse and buries his head in the ground, still thinking that the bomb will drop.

He finally looks up to see that they are on a metal balcony overlooking New Brassport. Next to Michael are The Redeemer and Cogsmire.

Michael: What is this? Where are we?

Michael says as he wipes tears from his eyes and stands.

Cogsmire: Well, you just so happen to be in the industrious society of New Brassport City, ole' bean. You'd ought count yourself lucky this splendid fellow here has one of Abraham's trademark stopwatches, or you'd be a dead man, mate. Ho Ho!

Redeemer: Consider this your second chance. A life away from earth… A new start.

Michael: Brother… I… I don't deserve this.

Redeemer: No… You don't. And I'm not your brother. My name is Ryan Martel. Your brother and I switched before… Never mind, I'll explain later.

Abraham: Hey kid… Remember me?

Michael starts to tremble as Abraham Williams himself walks toward him. To Michael's surprise, Abraham is still alive. Even more confusing, he seems to be more metal than human.

Michael: How are you still alive? I don't understand... I saw you die years ago!

Cogsmire: Oh please... Like a few bullets will stop the great Abraham Williams.

Abraham: I'm still here kid. And for some reason, so are you. Ryan? Care to explain?

Drake says nothing for the longest time.

Martel: So, for the past six months, me, your brother and Abraham have been living in New Brassport.

Drake: My brother… Can I see him?

Michael: Yes you can, Drake.

Michael and Abraham step out of the shadows of the room after staying there until the moment was right.

Drake: Brother! Wait!

Michael goes to hug Drake, but stops when he sees him grab the handle of his gun blade.

Drake: Is it true? Have you really changed?

Michael: I promise I have, Drake. I promise! I am no longer a slave to evil.

Drake: Even if that's so, you've killed a lot of people. People close to me! Justin's death is on you! All of those students at Orion City High School - you killed them and laughed! You still have to pay for that. Even if you've repented, there are still consequences.

The four men in the room stay silent as the tension builds.

Michael: And I plan to pay for my actions. I've been in prison this whole time, and my sentence is far from done, even here on earth.

Drake releases his grip from his gun blade. This moment for Drake is the first moment he sees his brother again - not the monster that he used to be. He grabs Michael and embraces him, and they both sob deeply.

Drake: Why didn't you just escape The Royale with me… You idiot!

Drake says this with love in his voice, and they both smile.

Michael: I didn't know what I was doing was wrong. I was so convinced that leading The Royale was my purpose.

I was so horribly wrong.

Abraham: He's been getting psychiatric help these past few months. He still has psychopathic tendencies and his powers are too great for him to just roam free. We don't want him turning out like Ronin.

Drake releases his brother's embrace and looks at Abraham.

Drake: Now I've heard how Ryan and Michael are here. But you… How are you alive? Chase needs to know.

Abraham: He can't know. Not yet.

Drake looks concerned over how Chase will take this, but eventually nods his head in agreement.

Abraham: The night I died… Well, the EMS took me away. Little did anyone know that the EMS technicians where citizens of New Brassport, my city. In the same way Ryan escaped, Cogsmire warped me back to my home, my real home. It took a lot of work, but they used all of the technology they had to fix me. That's why I look like a walking machine.

Drake: So, Cogsmire knew all of this?

Martel: Sure did. And we made him swear to secrecy, so that's why this is all news to you.

Abraham: It's a good thing too. He wouldn't have made it if I didn't save him last minute. I'm the reason he made it out of New Brassport the other day when the city was crumbling around us.

The room goes quiet once again. Never before had Drake experienced being in a room full of people who were supposed to be dead. Himself included.

Martel: But the reason we're here is to talk about the thing that started this whole mess. The Power Diamond.

Drake: The Power Diamond is with Gridd. I just sent him off to find Cody. Once they find him, they're going to find Silver.

Martel: Let's run down the whole timeline of this thing, shall we? The Power Diamond started in Jettahawk. That's where they protected it.

Michael: Then the Master Royale before me went to Jettahawk and stole the diamond - and the girl.

Drake: Yeah, Cody isn't going to be happy about that.

Michael ignores this and keeps talking.

Michael: The Royale kept the diamond for a while, until…

Abraham: I left New Brassport and lived on earth, protecting the diamond. Then The Royale stole it again… from me.

Drake: Then eventually my team and I took the diamond and Silver back.

Ryan: But the Royale had brainwashed and trained Silver into thinking she was Gladstone, just for the Guns of Abraham to find out…

Abraham: Gladstone was really Contra.

Martel: Right, but back up a bit to Judgment day. The portal Ronin escaped in was a portal Michael formed.

Michael: It was a portal I opened to escape. I didn't have time to focus on where I would escape to, so it opened a random location which just conveniently happened to be New Brassport.

Martel: Shortly after Ronin escaped, I dropped the Power Diamond into the portal. Leaving it with Ronin. Not my best move, I'd say.

Abraham: Ronin warped the diamond to Gladstone.

Drake: And soon Cody will find Silver.

Martel: That's what it looks like, yeah. A lot rides on them finding her.

Drake: I have faith that they will. Gridd misses his sister - and Cody… well, he won't stop until he finds her.

Martel: I just hope he can snap her out of the mental state she's in. The Royale is gone, but she probably still feels the need to serve the remaining leaders because of how badly they brainwashed her. It's truly sad.

Drake: Cody never lost faith in her. Not once. She's the reason he's not afraid to be Wolfbane anymore. That alone proves she has a connection in her heart with Cody. That should snap her out of it.

Michael looks very ill as he thinks about how much of this was his fault.

Drake: I still don't understand why you're all here. Why is now the time to tell me all of this?

Ryan looks at Michael and nods.

Michael: Because there is a bigger threat coming. Something much bigger than The Royale, or Torchwood, or even the Power Diamond.

Michael reaches in his pocket and hands Drake a note.

Written on the note is the name "Shadowlurk."

Drake: Shadowl..

Martel: Don't say it!

Drake is startled by this.

Drake: I don't understand.

Michael: When I became the Master Royale, it was just me, Torchwood, Gladstone, Clark, and Gresham. Torchwood would always talk about this leader of a place called the Dark Dwelling.

Drake: You mean?

Martel: Yes... The place Dusk is from.

Michael: He is the holder of all evil and he plans to take it out on Sky World first, and then Earth.

Drake: How do you know this?

Michael: Torchwood actually was crazy enough to try and communicate with him. To our surprise. It actually worked. And let me tell you, they talked regularly. I didn't believe myself until Dusk showed up. Dusk was proof that the Dark Dwelling existed.

Martel: And Dawn was proof that Sky World existed.

Michael begins to shake in fear, his voice trembles as he speaks.

Michael: He's coming to earth, Drake… And he's mad. He's coming to finish what Dusk didn't. And if Sky World can't stop him, it's up to us to stop him.

Abraham: And we will! I ain't letting no one take over earth. I already lost most of my true home. I'm not going to lose this one too.

Martel: Drake, if we're really going to do this, we have to prepare, and bring everyone we know together to fight. And for me…

Ryan zips up his brown Watcher cloak and places the hood on his head. He reaches in his pocket and pulls out three of his old throwing knives.

Martel: …it means going back to my roots.

Drake and Abraham smile at the sight of Ryan Martel in his true form. A determined guy in a brown hood.

Drake: Wait until Josh sees this… Ha ha! He's gonna freak out.

The four men look around at each other, determined and ready to fight Shadowlurk when he comes. This round table of men stands proudly together as a boy who escaped The Royale and made it his mission to eradicate them, a man who gave everything to bring his parents' killer to justice, a man who left the city he built to protect the diamond and keep his son safe, and a man who was once evil, doing all he can to redeem himself.

Ryan Martel

Abraham Williams

Drake Barrows

Michael Barrows

These are the men who represent all stages of redemption, and soon, they will prove to the world that redemption is possible, even when the most evil of beings attacks.

Martel: And Drake… You know what this means for you?

Ryan reaches behind him and places on the table a familiar red and black mask that Drake once wore.

Martel: It means it's time for The Redeemer to return to Orion City.

Drake picks up the mask and holds it in front of him. He looks at it as if were an old friend. Drake places the mask on his face after months of not knowing its whereabouts.

Drake exits the room and walks onto the balcony, within the main living area of the mansion.

Ryan follows him.

Teddy, Josh, Noah, Isaac, Tristen, Drew, and Zack look up at the two iconic figures on the balcony above them.

Josh looks up in shock as he sees the familiar brown attire Ryan used to wear.

Josh: Ryan! Is it really you?

Martel: Hey bud… Looks like you turned out to be pretty great, just like I said you would.

The two grin at each other as Josh looks completely astonished.

The rest of the team looks in amazement at Drake.

Dusk: Welcome back, Redeemer. Your team missed you…

Steampunk: Okay, I'm here…

Gideon stands at a table in a dark room. He turns around, revealing his red and blue eyes.

Behind him open two bigger red and blue eyes.

Gideon: Chase, I've seen the future of The Redeemers.

Their fate is inevitable.

STEAMPUNK AND GIDEON WILL RETURN

I'm Still Here

It's Never Over

Seth is dead.

See you soon.

53. 55. 106. 193. 166.

—Ronin Torchwood

Made in the
USA
Columbia, SC